ORIGINS

What Reviewers Say About Jen Jensen's Work

Jamis Bachman, Ghost Hunter

"I love ghosts. I love ghost hunter shows. And I loved this book. ...Jamis is a sarcastic woman with a bit of an ego despite her internal struggles with simply dealing with life. She was a messy and complex character that I couldn't get enough of. ...There were some intense moments. Great characters and friendships. A cute little romance. Crime solving mystery. Definitely worth your time."—*Bookvark*

"Jen Jensen weaves a fascinating story, fast-paced and gripping, with just the right amount of twists to keep me captivated." —*Jude in the Stars*

The Politics of Love

"It is now official. I always fall for the emotionally intense stories. And I totally fell for The Politics of Love. I love how The Politics of Love is not just a romance, but also a story with great conversations that spark thoughts. ...This beautiful work had my heart tingle in all the right places."—*Hsinju's Lit Log*

"Truly a great story that tackles a lot about not just coming from different political views but also on different lifestyles. I enjoyed the refreshing read because it is way out of my comfort zone. I don't usually read Political related themes in books, but I find *The Politics of Love* amazing."—*HeyYoItsDeej Blog*

Visit us at www.boldstrokesbooks.com

By the Author

Jamis Bachman Mysteries

Jamis Bachman, Ghost Hunter

Origins

Politics of Love

ORIGINS

by
Jen Jensen

2021

ORIGINS

ISBN 13: 978-1-63555-837-1

THIS TRADE PAPERBACK ORIGINAL IS PUBLISHED BY
BOLD STROKES BOOKS, INC.
P.O. BOX 249
VALLEY FALLS, NY 12185

FIRST EDITION: MAY 2021

CREDITS
EDITOR: CINDY CRESAP
PRODUCTION DESIGN: SUSAN RAMUNDO
COVER DESIGN BY TAMMY SEIDICK

Acknowledgments

If this book is good, it's with great thanks to Cindy Cresap. Thanks for taking a chance on me.

Dedication

To my grandmothers.

PROLOGUE

October 31, 2003

Jamis felt a twinge in her stomach, then a hand on her shoulder and heard a faint cry. She spun toward it. There was nothing behind her but an exquisite view of Jerome, Arizona. Old buildings were transformed into art studios, hotels, and restaurants. The town was built up and down mountains, perched on the edges of declines so sharp a wrong step meant death. The early settlers were brave to build in such a place. Time and modernity had softened its edges, made the roads into town more manageable, and the pathways safer. But it still felt perilous, as if a wrong step could end it all.

The sun had set just a few minutes before. It was not dark and it was not light. Her vision had not adjusted. There was no one behind her. Had she felt something? Or was it her overactive imagination? She should keep walking, get dinner with Maggie, go to bed, enjoy her vacation. Not create problems where there were none. Maggie would accuse her of sabotaging their one weekend away in over a year. It wasn't intentional. Jamis couldn't always control her moods.

She'd ask if Maggie heard something. If not, it was her mind, making something out of nothing. Not being able to trust her own mind and perceptions hurt.

"Did you hear something?" Her gaze was fixed on the distance.

Maggie continued up the road and turned around. "No, why?"

"You didn't hear someone call for help?" Maggie had not even noticed she was no longer next to her. What was she doing with her? She was afraid to let go. It was a humbling thought.

"No. Don't do this. I just want a nice weekend." Maggie came toward her. "Please."

"I'm not doing anything. I'm confirming," Jamis said.

"Well, it's confirmed. I heard nothing." Maggie's eyes flashed with something, and to Jamis, they looked hard. Jamis saw it and turned away. Maggie was always certain about her thoughts, feelings, and perceptions. Everything was order, control, and reason. It was exhausting.

Jamis didn't acknowledge Maggie's opinion. If she didn't want it, then why did she ask? "I just thought I heard something."

"Well, you didn't. This is the stuff I'm talking about. You really need to find someone to help. I'm concerned about you hearing and seeing things," Maggie said.

"Yeah, well, so am I," Jamis said. There was this sensation, somewhere between her navel and breastbone, that made her feel like someone needed her. It felt like an urge to move, swerve in traffic, or jump. They continued to the hotel in silence.

"I think it's because you didn't know your mom was dying. This feeling you have that people need your help." Maggie pushed into the door with her shoulder. The lobby of the hotel was dark, lit only by faux oil lamps. Their steps echoed and the wooden floors creaked. Jamis paused to look at a black-and-white photo on the wall. It was a group of coal miners posed in front of a mine, circa 1885. Their faces were blackened with soot and hardened with labor.

"Are you going to respond?" Maggie waited by the reception desk, hand next to the bell, waiting to summon help.

"Probably not. Not in the mood to psychoanalyze why I'm so damaged," Jamis said. She should tell Maggie it was better they go home, split up now.

"I didn't say that. I'm just suggesting these things you see have a root in observable phenomena," Maggie said.

"Thanks, Dr. Maggie. I'll keep that in mind."

"Jamis," Maggie said, but before she could continue, Jamis interrupted.

"Don't. Just get our room. Let it go." Jamis left her in the lobby and explored the lower floor of the hotel. The long hallway was lined with photographs and antique couches. She bent to sit on one and felt like she was going to fall, it was so low to the ground. It was probably not intended for a six-foot-tall person. Humans were not quite as big in the 1800s. Antibiotics, vaccines, and modern farming practices made Jamis a lot bigger than her human ancestors, and she was grateful for them, even if she felt like a giant, knees bent almost up to her chin.

The mirror on the wall across from her reflected her angst back. There were dark circles under her eyes. Her skin was pale, and her black eyes looked like deep caverns in her face. Maybe Maggie had good cause to be worried.

She'd not slept well in months. Her mother's constant presence in the corner of her bedroom made rest difficult. She fled to Maggie's apartment to sleep, until her mother followed her there a few weeks before. Her mental state was deteriorating, and Maggie knew it. Maybe this antagonism she felt for Maggie was a projection of her own terrible state. She was a mess.

Maybe she should pay attention. She looked terrible. She undid her ponytail and tied her hair back in a loose bun. She'd rest tonight. Sleep. Try to be kinder and more present with Maggie. Think about getting some help when they got back home. Enjoy the scenery. Jerome was rich with vivid architecture, nature, and history.

The dark carpet caught her attention. Swirls of faded color mixed in with dark red. It was probably striking once. She heard the low murmur of Maggie's voice and left the couch, drawn to a painting at the end of the hall. It was a portrait of a man and woman. The man was nondescript. He was an average white man in his late fifties, with sandy brown hair. But the woman was striking, with dark black hair and bright blue eyes. There was something familiar about her. Jamis stared and put her hand on the plaster wall to lean closer to the painting. Was there a flash in her eyes, behind the blue?

Then the wall gave way and disappeared and Jamis stood on the edge of the hill, a sharp incline below her. A man ran toward her and she froze. There was fog outside and it was day, not dusk. A figure wearing a long black dress trailed behind and then swallowed him, somehow, pulling him into her. The figure stopped at the bottom of the incline and looked up at her. For a moment, it was hundreds of feet away, and then it was right in front of her face.

Jamis screamed and jerked backward, threw her backpack at it and stumbled back to the middle of the hallway, trying to find solid ground. There was still no wall. A vague outline of a man was present inside the dark figure. Jamis heard screams and they abruptly stopped. The figure threw back the black veil covering its face, but Jamis couldn't see it. Darkness swirled around its head.

Jamis scrambled away, crashed into the wall, and fell into Maggie who raced toward her.

"My God. What's wrong?"

"Go, get out of here. The wall is gone," Jamis said, pushing her forward. Maggie refused and moved down the hallway.

"What are you talking about?" Jamis ran into the lobby. The wall was there, the figure gone.

"There was something there. And the wall disappeared," Jamis said. Maggie sighed, picked up the backpack, and went up the stairs. "Did I break you?" Jamis called after her, but Maggie ignored her. Jamis watched her go and closed her eyes. When she opened them, the figure was back and lifted its hand to the space where a mouth should be, like it was blowing a kiss. Then it flickered out of existence.

The painting on the wall glowed for a moment, moved from side to side, then rested, askew.

There was something there and Jamis knew it. Something had just happened to her and she'd find out what it was. Jamis followed behind Maggie, a new certainty inside. She wasn't crazy. She'd prove it.

Chapter One

The floor under her feet split and Jamis dropped. She hit the dirt below with a thud and a groan. Dust fell from above and she closed her eyes and mouth to avoid it. She rolled to her side, pulled her knees up to her chest, and held still. After a few moments, Jamis opened her eye closer to the ground. There wasn't much to see. After a few more moments, she opened her other eye, relaxed her legs, let her knees drop, and rolled onto her back. The floor above had split under her weight. Pieces of wood dangled above her and she shimmied to the right, out from under them in case they fell.

The room around her was dark, but light from above made a path in front of her. She pulled her iPhone from her pocket and turned on the flashlight. There was an open doorway, and dust covered crates and shelves filled with bottles of alcohol. Lanterns hung on the wall. She pushed to her feet and grabbed her side. Her ribs, just freshly healed, screamed with pain. For a terrifying moment, she was afraid they were broken again. As she caught her breath, the pain lessened, and then disappeared into a dull ache.

Now on her feet, Jamis spun around the room with her phone light. She'd fallen into a small room underneath the tunnel she'd impulsively decided to visit.

"Go visit one of Sage Creek's tunnels, I said. That will be so much fun. I need to get out of the house." Jamis spoke out loud to the empty space and brushed dirt from her clothes with her hand. "I did not say, oh, gosh, today I want to plummet what," she looked above her, "ten feet at least. Why does this shit happen to me?"

She wiped dust from her clothes and walked into the path of light shining from above. There was a larger group behind her. The tour guide recognized her. "Oh, I can go alone. Is that okay? I'm a professional, after all," she said to the empty space around her, repeating what she'd told him.

"Help," she cried upward, hoping they'd hear her.

She pointed her flashlight at the doorway. She could text Johnna, her girlfriend of just three months, but didn't want her to know she'd fallen. She queried up the chain of text messages with Sapphire, her friend and the town archivist. She'd met her a few months earlier and together, they solved a twenty-five-year-old murder. It involved a poltergeist, Johnna's mom, and ended up with Jamis in the hospital. But she'd met Johnna, Sam, and Carmen, and possibly, for the first time in her adult life, a family.

Help. I've fallen in the tunnel beneath the old Woolworth building. I think someone will come, but if they don't, can you please rescue me? She hit send. She had just one bar of service and held her breath as the blue line crossed the top of the screen. She smiled when it showed sent, the message traveling the ether to Sapphire.

Then there was a tall figure in the doorway about ten feet from her. One moment she was alone and the next, she wasn't. "Well, hell," she yelled as she jumped back and turned the light on the figure. It looked like a man, over six foot four, in a long, dark coat, with a tall hat.

"Who are you, Abraham Lincoln?" He didn't move. "Are you a person or a ghost?" Still no movement. She walked toward him, flashlight up. The light fell on his eyes and they glowed red. He smiled, his lips curled up and back, showing his moss covered green teeth. He lurched forward and opened his mouth. A black cloud emptied from it, like water falling from a bucket, and then swirled around him like a cloak. Jamis screamed.

The dark figure moved toward her in a fluid movement of shadows and smoke. She felt him settle over her like a hand covering her mouth, trying to suffocate her. She gasped for air and her knees buckled. Her phone dropped as she fell. Frigid cold seeped into her bones and she flailed against it and struggled to stand. Her sore ribs screamed again.

Jamis closed her eyes against the assault and centered her breath in her stomach and thought about Johnna. Thought about climbing from the guest bed over a month ago and sliding into her bed. Jamis hadn't slept alone since. She thought about their legs tangled in bed the night before, talking about their next day. She'd told her she was going to get out of the house, take a walk, look at the tunnels as they opened for summer. Jamis thought about Johnna climbing from bed to run, the sound of the shower running later, and the kiss she'd given her before leaving for the day.

Johnna, she thought, and pushed up to her feet. The dark cloud flew off her, as if in pain, and resettled back into the figure in the doorway. "What am I doing down here? I could be doing anything. Why am I down here with you?"

She shook her arms and kicked out her feet. "What the hell were you doing to me? That was so rude." He shimmered in and out of phase and then solidified. "I have an amazing girlfriend. She saves animals and doesn't eat them. She has these long legs, muscular from running, and she cooks. She always smells good, has an adorable dog, and operates on kittens. And I'm down here with you?"

The figure rose up in the doorway, creating wind that raged at her. Jamis jumped up and down, pumped her arms in front of her. "Oh no you don't. I've been through this before. I've been avoiding getting myself into these situations. I'm so bored I can't stand it, but I'm abstaining. Now, here you come. I don't think so. Shut up. Your hat is stupid," Jamis said and threw dirt at the figure.

It raged toward her before pulling back to disappear into the hallway from where it came. She jumped up and down. "God damn. That was scary." She lifted her head to the hole in the floor and screamed, "Someone help me."

"Oh my God, ma'am, are you all right? Where are you?" A young man crouched down on his hands and knees. It was the tour guide who'd let her go ahead. His head cast a shadow in front of her.

"I fell through the floor, and now I'm under it. That's where I am. Please get me out," Jamis said.

"I have to call nine-one-one. I don't know how to get you out." Jamis covered her face with her hands. The paramedics in town were going to get sick of her. "Don't go anywhere. I'm calling right now."

"Where would I go?" she asked and glanced at the open doorway. It was empty.

❖

The fire department had stuck a ladder down in the hole and she climbed out. For her drama, it was pretty anticlimactic. Sapphire rushed in just as a firefighter helped her from the ladder. She fussed over her for nearly twenty minutes before she was satisfied Jamis wasn't injured again, and then left to return to work.

Jamis fled the scene, even though photos were likely already blowing up social media. Buzzfeed probably had a story: "Famous ghost hunter Jamis Bachman, formerly of television show *Ghastly Incidents*, saved from a cellar in Sage Creek, Utah, just months after nearly dying while wrestling with a poltergeist!"

She was driving Johnna's powder blue 1980 Ford Bronco, and climbing into it made her feel a little bit better. It was just cool, and after being helped from a hole in the ground by a dozen firefighters, she needed cool.

Jamis glanced in the rearview mirror and jumped. There was a woman in a white bonnet in the back seat. Her skin was grayish green and cracked in the middle of her forehead and on her left cheek. Jamis could see her teeth through the hole in her skin. Black tears ran from her eyes. She opened her mouth but no sound came out. Jamis spun around in the seat. There was no one there. She hit the steering wheel with her fists.

"Holy hell." A couple on the street stopped to look at her. She smiled and waved. "Ghost in my back seat," she said and put the Bronco in drive. It didn't have air conditioning or she'd roll the windows up to avoid having to explain anything to anyone.

At the stop light, she glanced in the mirror. The woman was back. "You're kidding me." She held eye contact. "You can't follow me home. You just can't. You have to get out of the car. I can come back and talk to you later, but you can't come to Johnna's house." The woman opened and closed her mouth. "I'll pull the car over." The woman screamed before unfurling from the back seat in a haze of blue. Her phone rang. It was Johnna. "You better go," she yelled out her window as the blue smoke retreated. She slid the button to answer. "Hi."

"Sapphire just told me you fell into an abyss of never ending darkness where a black cloud tried to assault you. Is that true?"

Jamis turned right. "Are you wearing scrubs?"

"Don't deflect," Johnna warned her.

"Really. It would be nice to think about."

"Yes, but don't get frisky. Someone just brought in a box of kittens and they're watching me. It feels wrong," Johnna said. Jamis laughed while thinking about Johnna's strawberry blond hair pulled on top of her head to keep it out of the way. "Really,

Jamis?" Her bright green eyes and perfect smile. "Are you still there?"

"I was thinking about your smile. I'll tell you about it when you get home. When are you coming?"

"Around six," Johnna said. It was almost three hours away. Johnna paused again, her even, calm tone soothing and peaceful. "An endless abyss is what she said."

"I'll see you when you get home, and I love you." She said this quickly and hung up the phone before Johnna could respond. What would she do if Johnna didn't say it back? A few moments later, her phone chirped. She paused at the stop sign to look at her phone. There were two texts from Johnna.

I love you too.

An endless abyss of darkness and black smoke?

Jamis replied. *I should have stayed home.*

But she was out now, amped up and needing company. In the few months since she almost died solving the murder of Stephanie Gardner, the poltergeist, and accidental death of Johnna's mom and brother, Jamis had turned inward and deactivated her social media. Her physical recovery was long and hard. Broken ribs were something she never wanted to experience again. The headaches from her concussion were confusing, and for a few frightening moments, she thought jaw surgery was in her future. When she'd stepped off the plane in Salt Lake City, Utah, in March she had no idea what was to come.

But Johnna had nursed her back to health with presence, love, and a place to stay. During that time, Sage Creek had become the closest thing to a home she'd ever known. Jamis asked Johnna daily if it was time for her to leave, but the answer was always no, not yet. By all logical considerations, it seemed too soon to live together. They'd just met, lived through a traumatic and tragic set of circumstances together. Jamis worried over the situation, even as she struggled to move on from it. Was Johnna repeating a pattern of caretaking with her? Was Jamis going to get restless and flee when she was well? The questions went unspoken, but they haunted Jamis. When she tried to talk about it, Johnna only said, "I choose to trust this process and us. I choose to trust you."

It was so genuine and earnest Jamis had a hard time accepting it. But she was trying. She checked in the rearview mirror for passengers. Without a lot of thought, Jamis decided to stop by and see Detective Daniels, check on the progress of Stephanie's case. She parked in front of the police station and trotted up the stairs, holding her ribs and bruised side. The receptionist behind the counter recognized her and picked up the phone to ring the detective.

Jamis waited by the front windows, watching the cars pass on the street, strangely soothed by the constant movement. The traffic wasn't heavy but it was steady. She didn't even miss Los Angeles, though she spent most of the last ten years there. The mountains surrounding Sage Creek were breathtaking feats of nature, blocks of rock cascaded across the horizon, like castles rising from the earth. The dirt was red, orange, tan, and brown. Sagebrush and pine intermingled. It was the most beautiful place she'd even been, and she panicked with the idea of leaving it and Johnna. The loss would be too much to handle so she would trust this and Johnna and learn from her example.

"Jamis," a voice spoke behind her and she spun to face it.

"Detective Daniels," Jamis said.

"Pete, please. What's up?"

"Just checking in," Jamis said.

"The wheels of justice move slow," Pete said.

"But they're moving?"

"Yeah. Your friend is coming down in a few weeks to help with the autopsy," he said.

"Maggie is coming?" Maggie, her ex-girlfriend and great lost love. Or so she thought for years until life showed her different.

"You didn't know?" Pete waved for her to follow him. She settled into a chair in his office.

"No, but we don't talk regularly," Jamis said.

"It just happened today, so I thought that was why you stopped by. Maybe you heard. I called her," Pete said.

"But not me?"

"Trying to avoid any impropriety, being cautious," Pete said, unapologetic. Jamis accepted it. "The bad news is we got a bit bogged down trying to exhume her body. That gave Dan Abbey and his attorney time to bury us in motions and suits. But we are there, finally."

Dan Abbey had participated in the murder of Stephanie Gardner and failed to destroy the evidence, leading to Jamis's final confrontation with him and Bobby Reynolds, the other perpetrator. Had it not been for Carmen, an acquaintance and now friend, she'd have died. Like so many small towns, the lives of those involved had intersected with the murder and Jamis's investigation. When Jamis tried to really understand the magnitude of all that happened, and the synchronicity that brought her to Sage Creek, she was humbled and overwhelmed.

Instead, she focused on something else. There was a photo on the desk of Pete with a woman and two kids. Jamis pointed. "Your family?"

He put the photo down on its face. "Used to be. Divorcing."

"Awkward," Jamis said.

"I should move the photo, but I can't stand the idea of it," Pete said. Neither one of them knew what to say. He changed the subject. "How's Johnna?"

"Good," Jamis said, smile wide.

"Probably shouldn't screw that up. Keeper," he said.

"Tell me about it," Jamis said. Then, spontaneously, "Want to hang out sometime?"

Pete made eye contact. "Are you bored?"

"Yeah, I am, totally," Jamis said, the honesty of her answer surprising her.

"Maybe get back to doing what you do. You do it well," Pete said.

"Does that mean you don't want to hang out with me?"

"I'm on the fence," he said.

"Should my feelings be hurt you don't want to hang out with me?"

He shrugged. "Not my problem."

Jamis laughed and purposefully knocked the cup of pens off his desk. "And that's not mine," she said and blew him a kiss. His laughter followed her out of the station.

Chapter Two

W hen Jamis arrived home, she showered and changed her clothes. She considered making dinner, but the stove was gas and Jamis continued to be intimidated by it. Instead, she called for Chinese delivery. She took four Ibuprofen and stretched out on the couch, wishing she had social media to scroll. Maybe the detective was right and it was time to get back to what she did. She turned on the television and drifted into a Netflix original.

Around six, the crunch of gravel in the driveway alerted her that Johnna was home. She moved toward the back door, unable to wait inside to see her, but stopped to check her appearance in the microwave glass. She'd cut her hair off during her recovery with a pair of scissors. It wasn't the best haircut, but it gave her some relief. Sapphire fixed it into a more attractive short style later and she liked it. She washed it and thought little else of it when she was done, the natural curls of her hair holding enough form that the cut actually looked hip.

When she'd not seen Johnna for any length of time and anticipated her arrival, her heart hammered. Outside, Virginia zoomed into the yard, did her business, and saw Jamis step outside. She ran at her, careening into her with so much force, they both stumbled. Jamis picked her up and Virginia licked her face.

"She had more manners before we met you," Johnna said.

Jamis laughed, put Virginia down, and took Johnna's hand, pulling her toward her. Jamis wrapped her arms around Johnna's waist.

Johnna held her face with both hands. "An endless abyss of darkness?" Jamis kissed her. "You're trying to distract me," Johnna said.

"Is it working?"

"Yes. But only momentarily," Johnna said.

"Just momentarily?"

"Fine," Johnna said, pliantly leaning into her. "Maybe I'll give you forty."

"Just forty?" Jamis said as she lifted Johnna up the stairs into the house.

❖

Jamis sipped her Diet Coke and shifted to be more comfortable on the couch. Now that a few hours had passed, she ached more from her fall. Johnna saw her grimace and rubbed her back, concern on her face. "Are you going to chase another poltergeist and almost get killed?"

"I mean, at least, I don't plan to. I'll never go back to the Woolworth's, I promise."

"What happened?" Johnna rubbed her back in slow circles and Jamis looked at her from the corner of her eye. Johnna smiled. "You're avoiding eye contact." Jamis grinned, and Johnna touched a dimple. "Come on."

"What if you think I'm crazy? I spent my whole adult life chasing ghosts and only found proof in spurts and spits. Now, I see them everywhere. I mean, I saw them before, but now it's different, constant. It used to be mostly pretend for ratings. Then, it was fun for social media. As much as I wanted proof, it never came. I was just running in place. Then, I meet you." Jamis paused, took a breath. "Now, I have something to lose."

Johnna kneaded her neck, sat forward, and wrapped her arms around her, chin on her shoulder. "I want you to share with me."

"I went ahead of the group, which wasn't a good idea." Johnna laughed, arms still around her, and Jamis told her the rest of the story.

"Are you sure you can let this go? This angry mean guy? All dark and smoky? Do you want to follow up on it?"

"I don't know," Jamis said. "I don't want to get sucked into anything. I was thinking about heading back to San Diego. I have an apartment there. All my stuff. I could move it here, get a place."

Johnna quieted, chin on Jamis's shoulder. "Is it too early to live together? Do you think?" Jamis shrugged, hands up. "I've never lived with anyone. Have you?"

"Yes. Once. It was a disaster. Mostly because I was a disaster." Johnna nodded, not pressing for more. She never pressed for more. Jamis sometimes wished she would, but it wasn't in her nature. If asked to describe Johnna, Jamis would say she "allowed." If Johnna needed to move a mountain, she wouldn't blow it up. She'd wait for water, wind, and time to erode the surface, assume there was life to be lived on the side where she stood, probably set the broken leg of a chipmunk, cure the blight of the forest trees, and then take a nap under one. Jamis pulled away from her, then turned to face her.

"I love you," Jamis said, her body heavy with emotion. The fall was scary, even if she responded cavalierly to it, but saying that was scarier. She felt vulnerable and scared but pressed ahead anyway. Johnna waited, perfectly still, watching her. "But I can do a lot of damage."

"Why do you suppose we think we have to be perfect to be loved?" Johnna's question made her want to cry. There were tears hidden behind her eyes, and probably more, buried deep inside the cavern of her chest where she shoved everything else. Honestly, was she evolved enough to be with someone like Johnna? Only someone with years of psychotherapy asked questions like that. Jamis needed to find a new therapist to stay equal.

She didn't want to ever hurt Johnna but knew she might. Hurt people hurt people. Was she healed enough to settle down with one person? Make a life somewhere? Jamis thought about Johnna's soft skin under her fingertips, the sound of her pleasure, the tenderness of their connection, and she opened her eyes.

"Where did you go?" It was another good question. Jamis's fears often careened around unexpected corners and met new friends.

She fought her way back to presence and to Johnna. "I don't want anyone else. I just want you," Jamis said, and felt exposed and tried to pull away, but Johnna reached for her, pulled her back, and kissed her cheek then mouth.

"I love you," Johnna said. "I've heard, though I can't be certain, that love doesn't have to be hard, horrible, and painful. I've heard some people just love each other. I mean, I have no experience. Most things in my life have felt hard, but this doesn't. I just want you and I want this." Johnna looked at her with such tenderness Jamis squirmed under her gaze. "I'm choosing to trust you. Regardless of what happens, you can know it's my choice. I'm not naive. I know what can happen in life. I know this bubble could burst. Life is impermanence."

Johnna had survived a car wreck that killed her mother and littler brother and paralyzed her twin. Jamis had just uncovered the truth of the accident. They'd talked about it at length when Johnna wanted to discuss it. Mostly, she wanted to know how Jamis made contact with her mother, Emma, sorting it through her mind, piece by piece. Jamis assumed they'd be talking about it the rest of their lives.

Jamis didn't know what to say, so she pressed Johnna down on the couch, the Chinese food containers forgotten on the coffee table. The back couch cushions somehow ended up on the floor and the setting sun cast shadows across the front room. Johnna arched under Jamis and called her name, pulling her up into her arms. "Stay here with me. You can go, just always come back."

❖

They left the couch after Jamis fell and knocked the food containers over. They put the leftover food away and walked up the stairs together, hand in hand, and crawled in bed to watch the full moon come up through the wall length windows in the bedroom. Jamis loved the space. Johnna was a minimalist, without knowing there was a name or trend against consumption and clutter. Her home contained only what she needed, except for an overabundance of books. The bedroom was no different.

An old wooden door hung on the wall as the headboard. There was a small dresser against the wall and a cast iron, claw foot tub in the far left corner, a shower to the right. The toilet was the only thing closed off in the room. Johnna told Jamis she'd taken a sledgehammer to the walls between the bathroom and bedroom herself. The room was constrained and she felt trapped. Johnna had extreme claustrophobia, which was why she didn't fly anywhere. It wasn't hard for Jamis to understand, given her past, but she made note of it, tucked it away as something to guard against.

Jamis shifted, and Johnna lifted her head. "Am I too heavy?"

"No. I just can't hold still." Jamis reclined against the headboard door, and Johnna rested against her chest, both of them facing the wall of windows.

"Go get your laptop," Johnna said and sat up. She pointed at the door. "Check social media. Do your thing."

"I'm trying this whole not being crazy thing. I think it looks good on me," Jamis said.

"You look good no matter what. Be you, Jamis. Since you've felt better I feel how restless you are. Just be you with me."

Jamis crawled out of bed. "It didn't take much to convince me." Her laptop was plugged in on the nightstand in the guestroom, where she'd left it when she deactivated everything.

"Ready?" she asked, and powered it up. Johnna rested her head on Jamis's shoulder. "Don't get mad if I have love letters in here. I get those," Jamis said. Johnna chuckled. Jamis opened her email and social media and cleared the notifications and browsed comments.

"Oh, someone likes you." Johnna pointed.

"Robert Beeder of Deer Park, Illinois, thinks I'm a self-serving dyke." She pressed reply and wrote under his comment, *Hey @Robert Beeder—Kiss your mom with that mouth? Xoxo—Jamis.* She posted the comments and said, "Watch." The notifications lit up, one after another. She posted, *I'm back.*

"You're so happy right now," Johnna said.

"I actually am. Thank you. Email. Let's see what email I have." Jamis loaded her email and hundreds flooded the screen. She scrolled through them quickly, accustomed to sorting. "Oh, here's one. A ghost lawnmower in the backyard at night?"

"Come on," Johnna said. Jamis waited for more. "No. I veto it. Move on."

"But is it real? I mean it might be worthwhile," Jamis said.

"Does it actually cut the grass?" Johnna's question was very pragmatic.

Jamis didn't know how to answer or what her expectation would even be in such circumstances. "I see your point. Okay. Moving on. What's next?" They read through the emails into the night, filing those with promise. Johnna liked the haunted mental institution in New Jersey, as it seemed the most promising. Jamis opened an email they both fell silent reading.

Dear Jamis,

I'm Charlie Griffith. I can't really believe I'm writing to you right now, but my sister says I have to.

I inherited a ranch from my aunt Jessica. She was my mom's oldest sister, who lived alone and hoarded. The property is almost three hundred acres. It's out off I-10 on your way to California from Phoenix, in that space between Blythe and Palm Springs where there is nothing. No gas stations. No rest areas. Nothing. I'll attach the GPS location to the bottom of my email. She left it to me and my sister, Gwen, in her will. I'm the executor. My mom died a few years back, and me and my little sister are all that's left of that family line.

I didn't know she was dying until the ambulance brought her into Phoenix to a hospital here and they called me. We didn't see her home until after she was gone and had to do something with it. We had no idea how bad it was. We decided to hire people to clean it out, and then once that was done, we planned to hire another company to demo it. We figured we'd just clear the land, leave the septic and power connections, and sell it for new build.

When I tell you the property was disgusting, I mean it. Her plumbing stopped working years ago. The people we hired had to hire subcontractors who wore hazmat suits to clean out her waste from buckets around the house. Honestly, I won't tell you much more about this because it's all cleaned up now, but it was like the whole house was a compost heap. In one corner, where she'd thrown a tomato, there was actually a tomato plant growing.

Me and Gwen had to drive out there while this process was underway. The guy running the crew said he'd never seen anything like it. They had about seven of those big haul-away trailers out there, and they had to take them away once and bring them back. Eventually, they got to the bottom of the pile. They power washed the house for me, inside and out. I hired a junk yard to come take away all the cars, and a company who specializes in metal recycling did the same with a bunch of other stuff. I hired a landscaping company to clear out all the overgrown brush. All told, this took about five weeks from start to finish.

Me and Gwen rode out there to see the finished product. We'd both seen it when we took possession of it and couldn't believe the transition. When we went inside the house, it was stripped bare. The biohazard company had ripped out most of the walls because of mold. They'd told me it was so bad the people doing the demo could actually get hurt if they were exposed to it. All bare like that, with everything gone, Gwen and I realized the house could actually be saved. What was cool was that we could see the original structure of the house and where it was added onto over the years. The house is probably about four thousand square feet. There's a guest house on the back of the property, and we cleaned that out too. It was probably once worker's quarters. It's about two thousand square feet.

We decided we'd see about selling it as is, and if we couldn't, we'd raise the funds to fix it and then sell it. The whole process had been such a nightmare, but now that we could see the potential of the place, both of us were excited. I contacted a bunch of Realtors, and they all agreed that we should install the basics in the house. We decided to do as much as we could ourselves.

This was when it all really started to get weird, though looking back, I think it might have started as soon as we took possession of the place. There was just an energetic change in my life. It got heavier, somehow. I thought it was the responsibility of the property.

I took my fifth wheeler out there and connected it to the power supply. Gwen and her kids came out on the weekends in their trailer. At first it was so much fun. We worked all weekend on the house, about six weekends in a row. Then, one Saturday afternoon, late, just as the sun began to set, my sister's oldest boy, Chad, yelled at us. He'd stumbled upon a door, hidden under some sagebrush on the back far side of the property. It was an old root cellar, but what we found in there was the stuff of nightmares.

That sounds so crazy.

But it's true. It was full of torture devices, like the stuff from the Middle Ages in dungeons? It freaked us out so we called the cops. A state patrol officer came out with a cop from Blythe. They said it was old stuff probably used in slaughter in the late nineteenth and early twentieth century. My sister thought maybe we should contact someone at ASU, but we didn't really know who. We closed and locked the room and decided to think about it.

But I think we let something out that night.

I was sleeping and the wind started howling and the trailer shook. That's common. I don't know if you've ever been out in the middle of the desert at night. Nothing people from the city can even understand. The darkness is complete, unless there's a moon. When the sun is up, you can see forever, the mountains look like mirages but they're real, you just never know how far away they really are. The wind blows a lot. I decided to get up and see if there was a storm coming. You can see the clouds coming in for miles.

So I walked out of my trailer and I saw something, I don't know what, hovering over the house. It was like this red cloud and it saw me. I don't know how a cloud sees someone, but this cloud did. I felt it look at me. I thought I'd die. All the air left my lungs and I felt like something sat on me. I fell to my knees and crawled across the yard to my sister's trailer. I banged on the door, hanging on to the metal fold down step to reach. She opened the door to find me lying on the ground, unable to breathe or move. She thought I was having a heart attack, but as soon as the light from inside the trailer hit me, I started to breathe again. I pointed at the house and tried to tell her what I saw, but it took about twenty minutes for me to be able to talk again.

We cleared out the next morning. She believed me because she wasn't feeling well either. We decided to just put the house on the market, get what we could, and be done with it. But it wasn't that easy because about one week later, I woke up in the middle of the night to see a guy standing at the bottom of my bed. Even when I turned the light on he stood there. He had on tan pants, a white shirt, and one of those old work hats. At first, I was really scared. But after a while, the newness of it wore off. He'd show up around one in the morning. I started waking up at that time, probably because I sensed him there. He just stood there, moving his lips, and then he leaves after about fifteen minutes. I told my sister about it and she came over one night.

We sat on my bed, ready for him to show up and he did. She screamed and ran from the room, but I felt braver because she was there and I wasn't crazy. So I stood up and walked to him and I heard what he was whispering. "She knows. She knows." Over and over again, that's all he says.

My sister is sitting here as I write this email. She used to watch your show. I'm hoping maybe you can help us like you helped those people in Utah. She showed me the news article about it. I'd really like this guy to go away. I'd also like to know what tried to kill me out at the house so we can get rid of it and sell that awful place and move on.

Thanks for your time. I'll add my phone number below too, so you can call me if you want. I swear I'm not lying. If you come down to Arizona, I can show you.

Sincerely,
Charlie & Gwen Griffith

"Wow," Johnna said.

"What do you think?" Jamis asked her, surprised by how important her opinion was.

"Either they've created an amazing story, or your next adventure awaits," Johnna said. Jamis pressed reply on the computer screen and started typing. "I love Arizona. If you go, I'll come visit." Jamis grinned and typed faster.

CHAPTER THREE

The walkway bridge connected to the plane, scraping against the metal. Jamis was cramped in a middle coach seat. At six foot, she folded up like a collapsing outdoor recliner to fit into airplanes. She wiggled, ready to get out. From San Diego, the flight to Phoenix was only forty-five minutes, but it felt longer. She'd gone back early the week before to deal with her apartment. She'd sent a single pod to Johnna in Utah, still unsure whether she should find her own space or just move in.

She tucked the thought away, content to think about it over time. She couldn't stop fidgeting.

"Oh my God, stop moving," Sapphire said. She'd insisted on taking the window seat so she could take pictures. Jamis was grateful because the only seat she hated worse than the middle seat was the window seat.

"I can't help it," Jamis said.

"You're almost forty. You can handle it." Sapphire had come to Los Angeles to purchase equipment for her archive in Sage Creek and stayed a few days to help Jamis settle her affairs. She couldn't resist taking a few more days off to chase a mystery with Jamis in Arizona.

"Okay, your legs are so short you still can't touch the ground. You have no idea what it feels like to be crammed in here," Jamis said. She turned and stretched her legs into Sapphire's space.

"See how tiny your legs are? I should have sat like this the whole flight."

"Move your legs. This is my space," Sapphire said, her tone dramatic.

"I thought you were a socialist. Does anything really belong to any of us? Isn't everything shared?" Jamis grinned, thrilled with her clever response.

Sapphire pulled a face at her and pointed at the door. "You're so pleased with yourself. Look, they're opening the door. You'll be able to unfold in a moment."

People began standing up on the plane, pushing into the center aisle, and Jamis joined. She pulled their carry-ons from the overhead compartment a few aisles in front of her.

"Oh my God, that's Jamis Bachman," someone behind her said. It was an older woman, with graying hair and heavy glasses. Her traveling companion smiled and Jamis winked at them and maneuvered up the aisle. The time off had been nice, but she needed movement and adventure.

"Not like that won't go to your head," Sapphire said, keeping pace with Jamis.

A blast of furnace-hot heat hit them when they stepped from the plane. Sapphire gagged and the flight attendant laughed. "Welcome to Phoenix." Jamis saluted and powered on. Inside the terminal, she leaned against a pillar and texted Johnna. She dialed Carmen's phone number.

Sapphire hooked her travel bag onto Jamis's rolling suitcase and grinned. "Thanks for pulling that for me."

Jamis began to protest but Carmen answered.

"Yeah?" There was muffled noise behind Carmen's voice. She said something else, but Jamis couldn't make it out.

"Where are you?" Like Sapphire, Jamis met Carmen in her last ghost hunting adventure. Carmen hired a manager for the grocery store she owned in Sage Creek and decided to travel more. She'd spent twenty-five years mourning Emma, Johnna's mom, and the love of her life. Something in her had come back to life that spring. Jamis asked her to meet them in Phoenix and she agreed.

"Waiting by your baggage claim," Carmen said.

"On my way." Jamis and Sapphire maneuvered through the busy terminal at Sky Harbor. Sapphire pointed at the milky waves of heat trapped above the earth as they rode down the escalator.

"Phoenix in summer is the hottest kind of hell there is," Sapphire said.

Jamis agreed quietly but felt happy to be back in the desert southwest. She loved Johnna and their little world but missed the sun. "Let's get Carmen, the rental car, and chase some ghosts," Jamis said.

Jamis accelerated onto the ramp for I-10 West, the Phoenix skyline in the rearview mirror. At three in the afternoon, the freeway was already congested, and they moved along in stops and starts, until it opened up to seven lanes outside the metropolitan area. Jamis settled into the left lane, drove eighty-five until she couldn't resist pressing the speed limit further. She decelerated at the sight of highway patrol cars as they left the city limits, breaking into the wide expanse of desert. Mountains shimmered in the distant landscape like mirages, the hot air dancing in front of them like waves. Like the mountains of eastern and southern Utah, these mountains erupted from the earth's crust with force, millions of years before as tectonic plates shifted.

"The landscapes of earth are all a result of force, gravity, and the random collision of moving parts. And we take them so seriously. Travel brochures. Names," Jamis said, pondering the desert. "Maybe that's just all of creation though. The big bang. That's just how stuff happens in this universe. Some creator out there says, 'Gonna throw a whole bunch of shit together and see what happens.' Suddenly, we've got everything from Netflix to the Bible, Twitter, Donald Trump, cancel culture, Halloween, and the Dollar Store."

"Walmart. I mean, I guarantee no creator thought of Walmart. They're as surprised as we are," Sapphire said. Jamis laughed.

"You two hurt my head," Carmen said.

"Ooh, but also, French fries. That has to be proof of some sort of harmonic convergence of synchronicity and divine inspiration, right?" Sapphire said, ignoring Carmen's protests.

"Spotify. And Amazon. I mean, come on," Jamis said.

"Fancy coffee. When these plates were crashing into each other millions of years ago, do you think some divine mind was like, 'Gonna set this up so someone can make soy lattes.' It's absurd. Just being alive," Sapphire said.

"Wanna stop for tacos? I'm hungry," Jamis said.

"I don't know if there is any grand purpose, but I love guacamole," Sapphire said, laughing.

"So, what are we doing now? Heading to the property?" Carmen interrupted them.

"Well, tacos at that Del Taco over there," Jamis said. Sapphire clapped. "But then, yeah. We have to find something. Narrow down our possibilities. Sapphire did some research beforehand about the property, but we didn't find much. We can get a hotel in Blythe, because it's close. Just gotta call Charlie, the property owner. He said he'd meet us there. What's there, I don't know."

"Well, you figured it out with Stephanie and Emma, so you'll probably figure this out too," Carmen said with calm reassurance. Jamis felt Carmen's trust and acceptance wrap around her and was comforted by it.

"Yeah, maybe it will just happen here too. I mean, I've been doing this a long time, but it's gotten really real since I've met all of you," Jamis said.

"Yeah, we're game changers. Now get me a taco," Sapphire said.

CHAPTER FOUR

Jamis called Charlie after they ate. Semis roared on the freeway in front of her. The wind blew hard and she pressed against the wall to muffle the sound when Charlie answered.

"Charlie? It's Jamis," she said, a little too loud. She looked around, but no one was paying attention. Carmen came out the door and toward her.

"Hey. I'm here and waiting for you," he said.

"Great. I'm just about twenty minutes from you. We stopped for food," Jamis said.

"Sounds good then. I'll be here when you get there. Holler if you can't find it," Charlie said, disconnecting the call. He wasn't as talkative as he'd been when they talked before she arranged to visit. But he'd told her the property made him feel uneasy, so she attributed it to that and moved on.

Sapphire appeared behind Carmen, sipping on a milkshake. "Dairy is evil," Jamis said.

"Wanna sip?" Sapphire held it out for her.

"Yeah," Jamis said, taking it from her hand.

"I'm telling Johnna," Carmen said. Jamis gave Sapphire the milkshake back, after taking a long drink.

"I got you churros," Sapphire said, holding a bag up for Jamis.

"Ma'am. I love ya," Jamis said.

The wind and freeway noise overloaded Jamis and she breathed deep, closed her eyes, and calmed her anxiety. Hiding away with Johnna was restorative and safe. She'd not felt this stimulated in months and had dropped all her coping mechanisms. She missed Johnna then and called. Johnna answered just as Jamis climbed in the car.

"Hey, I hope you're not busy," Jamis said.

"Just heading into surgery. But I have a minute. All okay?"

"Yeah. I had a sip of a milkshake, I'm sorry, and now we're heading to the property. About twenty minutes out." Jamis turned on the car.

"Be careful. Let me know how it goes?"

"I will. I love you," Jamis said.

"Love you too. I'll call you later," Johnna said.

"Ah, so sweet. My heart," Sapphire said. She feigned collapse against the door. "I love the two of you so much."

Jamis blushed. Carmen rubbed her forearm. "Okay, let's go get this bread," Jamis said, her new favorite catchphrase with Sapphire.

"Cuz we already got the taco," Sapphire said.

"No, you were supposed to turn," Carmen said, holding up the phone.

"How can I turn there? There was nothing there," Jamis said, agitated and exasperated. The car lurched into holes and they jostled uncomfortably in their seats.

"I think she's right," Sapphire said. "Mine shows you should have turned too."

"I bet Google hasn't even been out here," Jamis said, pressing on the brake. "I'm throwing it in reverse." She turned, arm around the back of Carmen's seat and backed up. She saw it then, the missing road. "Fine, never say I'm not open to feedback."

The road was as rough as the one before and dust filtered into the vents. Jamis turned off the air. "For a minute," she said. Carmen and Sapphire agreed. The ground was so dry the dust in front of the vehicle was like a sandstorm and visibility was low. It was disconcerting to be so removed from civilization. Jamis shivered, uncomfortable, deep unease spreading through her middle. There were no competing sounds to the crunch of tires and the sound of her heart beating.

"You okay?" It was Carmen, hand on her arm.

Jamis nodded, dropping in speed. "Yeah, just have a bad feeling."

"Okay, you can't say stuff like that," Sapphire said. She covered her eyes and peeked at Jamis through her fingers. "Like what?"

"Deep, paralyzing dread?" Jamis opened her mouth to say something else when the house came into view.

Jamis slowed the car then parked a few hundred feet from the house and a man who waved wildly at them.

"I assume that's Charlie," Carmen said.

"Yeah, me too," Jamis said, fighting an urge to flee. How irresponsible would it be to throw the car in reverse, speed off down the road, find the first flight out and pretend this never happened? But then Carmen opened her car door, suddenly social and friendly on the other side of the last adventure.

"Well, hi there," she yelled, long strides carrying her to the man.

"God damnit," Jamis said.

"What?" Sapphire paused, half in and half out of the car.

"I was thinking about leaving and now I feel obligated," Jamis said.

"Come on. You'll feel better after we check this out," Sapphire reassured her. Jamis climbed reluctantly from the car, unsure of her new hesitation. She felt afraid and realized that it was because now she had something to lose. She used to race into situations, never pausing to consider the ramifications, but now, there was Johnna, Virginia, and her friends. Really, finally, the orphan had found her family. She sucked the tears back into her eyes, a practiced movement, and concentrated on her swagger. She needed to get her edge back.

Charlie pumped Sapphire's hand up and down and then rushed to her. "You're Jamis, I know. My sister showed me your picture. She's just using the bathroom in the RV and will be right out."

"Good to meet you," Jamis said. The door to the RV opened and a middle-aged woman walked toward them. Her hair was gray and her eyes dark, unlike Charlie's blue eyes and blond hair, but despite those differences, they looked just alike.

Gwen came toward her, all smiles, and rushed to shake their hands, thanking them profusely for coming to help. "I was such a fan of your show and follow you on Facebook," Gwen told Jamis. She added, emotion gushing, "You're so brave."

Jamis grinned, always the same way when someone appreciated her. "But I don't feel too brave. I didn't want to get out of the car," Jamis said, looking around. "Something doesn't feel right here. Something makes me want to run."

"See?" Gwen pointed at Jamis, staring at her brother. "She is the real deal. Legit. Like a psychic or something."

"I wouldn't go that far," Jamis said. "Maybe highly sensitive and hypervigilant." Everyone fell silent. Maybe Jamis had high sensitivity synapses, an observable trait in many mammals. Her early life trauma and abuse took what was innate and amped it up, like she was constantly on prednisone. She noticed everything, even when she wasn't consciously aware of it. "I can't always identify what I'm noticing so it manifests in this kind of free-floating terror I have right now."

"Are you okay?" Sapphire's hand was on her arm. She'd moved to Jamis's side.

"Yeah." Jamis nodded. "I'll just push through it. Let's take a look around. Show us everything."

Charlie waved them forward and looked relieved to escape the conversation they were having. Gwen settled next to Jamis's other side. Jamis felt the warmth of Sapphire, drew from it, and calmed. Carmen strode ahead, next to Charlie, chatting about the property.

Charlie stopped, pointing to a spot just in front of them. It was a fifth wheel RV connected to electricity and water. What looked like a sewer drain ran to a hole in the ground and Jamis assumed it was a septic system. "I put the trailer right back where it was for you. When I came out and thought I was being suffocated." Jamis walked to the spot and turned around in circles. There was nothing but skyline. Mountains obscured by hot air in the distance. Sagebrush. Desert dirt. The RV behind her.

They followed him to the side of the house. He pointed behind it to an orange flag on a stake in the ground. "That's the room I told you about. With the weird stuff. State trooper said not to go back down there last week, until they figure it out. So you can't go, sorry."

"Sure," Jamis said. She'd go when Charlie left.

Jamis motioned Charlie forward to the house. It was gutted, just as he said. The basic shape of the house was visible, but it was just boards and cement. Jamis stepped in through what was likely the front door. It was a spacious ranch house.

"You should have seen this place when we got it," Gwen said.

"Yeah?" Carmen turned to Gwen, clearly interested.

"Our aunt was a hoarder. I've never seen anything like it," Charlie said.

"Just the stuff of horror movies. Like you can't even process someone living this way. Unless they're really crazy, out of touch," Gwen said.

"Or if someone is making them crazy," Jamis said.

"What do you mean?" It was Gwen.

Jamis stood still, right in the middle of the space. The wind outside picked up. A small dust cyclone spun to life and then dissipated. Something crept up her leg. It felt like vines growing from the ground, wrapping around her ankles, calves, thighs, holding in her place. Movement was impossible. Life felt futile. "We are born just to die," she said, staring at her feet.

"Okay," Sapphire said, eyes wide with alarm. "Um, what's going on?" Carmen leaned against the wall. Charlie and Gwen didn't move and stared at her with shocked expressions.

"Life is meaningless. So is death. Nothing matters. It's all a black expanse of nothingness. Why care? Why move? It's better just to rest." Jamis sat on the floor.

"Jamis, get up," Sapphire said and grabbed her arm. Jamis waved her away.

"Wait," she said and fell back on the exposed cement. The back of her head struck the ground and pain ricocheted. It didn't matter. Nothing did. A dark tunnel opened above her. Flashes of red light reached from it and Jamis lifted her hands to touch it.

"Jamis, get up," Sapphire said, pulling her arm. Jamis ignored her.

To the right, another small dust cyclone swirled to life and moved toward them in the house. A car alarm blared. Charlie put his arm around Gwen and fished around his pocket for keys, trying to silence the alarm. Carmen stared at the cyclone, not moving. Then the sun was gone. Clouds rolled across the sky and there was a thunderclap. Jamis closed her eyes. Her head hurt and nothing mattered.

"Nothing matters," Jamis said.

"Everything matters," Sapphire said, tugging Jamis's arm.

"No. We all die," Jamis said.

"Johnna matters. And Virginia," Sapphire said.

Jamis opened her eyes and looked at Sapphire. "Johnna."

"Yes, Johnna. Now get up!"

But a demon with red eyes and hands with long blades sat on top of her. She saw it now and met its eyes and it smiled at her, teeth yellowed and covered in dried blood. "Jamis," it said. "Stay here with us. You'll like it."

"Jamis, goddamn it," Sapphire screamed. Jamis ignored her, fixated on the being on top of her chest. "Carmen, get over here!"

Carmen jerked away from the wall, seemingly more alert. Jamis looked at her so she didn't have to look at the demon on her chest any longer. Was it a demon? Should she ask?

"What are you?" The thing laughed at Jamis and bared its teeth.

"Pretty. Aren't I pretty?"

"No. Are you a demon?" Jamis tried to touch it, but it turned to smoke as her fingers passed through it and solidified again when her arm fell back to the ground.

Carmen grabbed Jamis's arm, and Sapphire took her other arm. Together, they tugged her upright, balancing her on their shoulders.

"Well, this is a trend," Carmen said.

"You're a burden to your friends," the demon said to Jamis. "So much work. So many issues." He touched her face with a long blade, just barely, as he clung to her neck. "We could love you though."

"Get me out of this house," Jamis said and closed her eyes.

"Is she bleeding?" It was Gwen. A trickle of blood ran down Jamis's face.

They crossed the threshold of the house and a gap in the clouds let the sun through. The dust cyclone dissipated. Jamis focused on the break in the cloud and pulled away from her friends. The demon let go and sat in front of her on the ground. "She's been waiting for you." Then it disappeared.

"Holy hell," Jamis said, bending over, hands on her knees. Carmen had let go of her but stood close.

"What just happened?" Carmen rested her hand on Jamis's shoulder, eyes soft with concern. Her kindness made Jamis want to cry. Carmen was always so honest and heartfelt, whether she was concerned or angry. Jamis saw maturity and presence in Carmen she wanted in herself. Would it be wrong to just hug her?

"I don't actually know," Jamis said, turning around to look at the house instead. She had to get her strength back. She couldn't be this emotional and needy all the time. "But a demon was just sitting on me. I felt absolute darkness and loss of hope."

"A demon?" It was Charlie, eyes wide.

"He had red eyes and long blades as hands." She told them what he said to her but left out its last utterance. She didn't want to admit anyone was waiting for her.

"You're bleeding," Gwen said, rummaging in her purse. She pulled out a handkerchief and handed it to Jamis who stared at it, uncertain. Carmen took it from her and put it on the cut. Jamis replaced her hand with her own.

"This is nuts," Charlie said.

"Any more nuts than that guy at the end of your bed?" Gwen challenged her brother. He put his hands up.

"Are you okay?" Sapphire lifted the edge of the handkerchief to look.

"I don't know. I recognize those were not my thoughts, but I'm not sure what to do with them now. I must have just scratched myself. Let's keep moving. Show me the rest of the property," Jamis said.

"Are you sure?" Charlie was concerned, face tense. He bit his lip.

"Yes, I am. It's been worse than this," Jamis said.

"That's true. I saved her from near death at the hands of a killer a few months ago," Carmen said.

"When you say it that way, I feel pretty awful," Jamis said. Carmen shrugged. But something in the distance caught her eye before she could ruminate much longer. It was a swirl of darkness that felt familiar. It pulled her forward and she began to run toward it, long legs eating up the earth, strides strong and confident, though her ribs ached with the exertion. She skidded to a stop about one hundred feet from where she began her sprint.

The figure rushed toward her and then stopped. There was a clang of metal against metal. It echoed. The sound pierced the air. Jamis covered her ears and turned to look at the others. Their hands were up as well. Charlie bent forward, hands tight on his head, in obvious pain. Then, there was a noise Jamis could only correlate to a sonic boom and the ground shook. She lost her balance, stumbled onto hands and knees.

"Jamis," she heard. A blast of wind kicked up dirt. "Jamis," a voice called out. She struggled to face her friends. Sapphire was yelling to her, trying to get to her. Jamis waved her back. Sapphire didn't listen and finally arrived by her side. "What the freaking bad tacos? It felt like I had weights on my ankles," Sapphire said and yanked Jamis to her feet. "I'm always making you stand up."

Jamis's balance was off, but she was steady enough to stand. The demon was back and sitting on a wall of stacked rocks, tail swishing. "Do I believe in demons?" Jamis asked Sapphire. Sapphire shrugged. The demon waved at her, long blades moving up and down in the air. It looked playful, happy. Its mouth moved but Jamis couldn't hear it.

"What? You got something to say, say it louder," she yelled.

The demon left its perch and charged at her. It happened so fast she had no time to respond. But she felt it pass through her body and then circle back to do it again. It stopped, right in front of her face, balanced on its tail. "How's your face?"

Jamis shoved it, felt cold damp flesh under her fingertips. It laughed and raced back, hiding behind the swirl of darkness.

"Stay here," Jamis said. She wanted that figure. She raced past the block wall and broke into a sprint, but the harder she ran, the farther away the figure moved until finally, it disappeared completely. She stopped, hands on her aching ribs, and surveyed the landscape. Sapphire was about one hundred feet behind her. She ambled slowly back to her, looking at the ground for evidence anything was there.

"What the hell? Was there just something in front of us?" Sapphire's hands were on her hips and her face ashen.

"The demon," Jamis said, almost back by her side. "And something else in the distance." They walked back to Carmen, Charlie, and Gwen. "What was that?" Jamis called out as soon as she was close enough.

"I mean, that wind is what happened that night I told you about. But that metal? And the boom? That I don't know," Charlie said.

"What were you chasing?" Gwen stared at them, eyes wide.

"I have no idea," Jamis said.

"Should we be worried? I mean, I just don't know," Charlie said.

"If it makes you feel any better, none of us know what's going on until we do," Jamis said.

"I'm not sure I understand," Charlie said.

"I mean, you don't know what you don't know while you're in the middle of it. You just got to keep moving deeper into the story and hope the answers come," Jamis said.

"A demon," Sapphire said, interrupting, tone unbelieving. "I didn't see it, really, just a flash of something."

"I mean, I'm calling it a demon, but maybe it's something else," Jamis said, turning to her.

"A demon?" It was Gwen.

"I think it's what made your aunt deteriorate. But it could be anything. A malevolent entity living in a different dimension. An alien. An ancient spirit of the desert. So many different possibilities. But it's vicious and dangerous."

Jamis had detached enough from her emotions that her heart rate slowed. She wasn't scared so easily, just out of practice.

Something or someone wanted to engage with her. The experience she just had was extraordinary. Inconceivable. Could she capture the demon on video? She could manage whatever was happening here. She was the living one, after all.

"Wanna stay the night out here?" She grinned at Sapphire and felt like herself, with the added security of being loved. It was a new sensation.

Chapter Five

I'm not staying the night out here," Carmen said again.
"Come on. Charlie said we can," Jamis said, pressing
the issue. They were all in the RV. It was surprisingly spacious.
Jamis had her eye on the bed up the small stairs. It would be
cool to look out at the stars from there. It would be even better if
Johnna was with her.

"I'm not sold on it, either," Sapphire said.

"You're my partner. You have to stay," Jamis said.

"Oh, you're together?" It was Gwen, beaming. The thought
obviously made her happy.

"Oh, no," Jamis said at the same time Sapphire began to
speak too. "I'm with her boyfriend's twin sister."

"But you're settled down?" Gwen asked, waiting for an
answer. Jamis was rendered momentarily speechless. "You're so
cute. I told Charlie I hope she has a girlfriend." Jamis blushed.
Carmen laughed. Charlie coughed. "That's my brother telling me
not to pry. I'm just such a fan."

"Jamis definitely has a corner on the adoring women club,"
Sapphire said.

Smiling, Jamis said, "It's certainly my burden." Gwen
laughed and swatted at her.

"Anyway, like I said when we talked the other day, you're
welcome to stay. It's why I brought the RV," Charlie said, cutting

in. "It's starting to get dark, so if you don't mind, I'm gonna get out of here. You want a ride to a hotel? There's one just up I-10. Don't mind taking you, either." He spoke to Carmen who nodded.

"Yeah, they can come get me when they're done doing whatever they're doing out here," Carmen said.

"Fine. Chicken," Jamis called after her as she followed Charlie down the steps. Carmen ignored her, chatting with Charlie. Gwen hugged Jamis.

"Please be careful," she said, letting go of Jamis to hug Sapphire. "Both of you. There's something out here. After what happened, is this wise?"

"No," Jamis said.

"It's idiotic," Sapphire said. They both shrugged.

They walked outside to watch the others leave. Carmen took her bag from the rental car and tossed Jamis the keys. She blew them a kiss as they drove away. The sun was dipping into the west, reaching lighted fingers across the sky in brilliant red and orange hues. The sky behind them was a deepening purple color and the clouds from earlier rolled north.

"He said there was coffee," Jamis told Sapphire. "Want some?"

"Yeah. And then I want to call Sam. Say hi," Sapphire said. Jamis made kissy noises at her as she followed her up the steps of the RV but stopped when a flash of black and red caught her eye.

Jamis backed down the stairs and stood at the end of the RV.

"You okay?" Sapphire's voice was faint.

"Yeah, go ahead and call Sam. Be right in," Jamis said. There was nothing in the distance. When she looked to the left, Charlie's car was barely visible. They'd disappear from sight in a few more minutes. The sunset was even more brilliant, but she was too anxious to enjoy it.

There was something behind that block wall. The thought was unbidden. Charlie hadn't said anything about it in his letter or earlier, but there was something there. Jamis followed her instinct, back out to the edge of the property. It was just beyond a barbwire fence, running in jagged, uneven lines. Now that she was closer, Jamis understood the stones were a wall that were part of a larger structure. It wasn't uncommon to see abandoned, delipidated structures throughout the desert southwest. People built them fast, and then moved on, looking for the next best piece of land, gold, or other treasure.

But this felt different, like it was part of something important. Jamis took a deep breath, stilled her thoughts, imagined roots running from her feet, into the ground, and stepped around the wall. There was nothing there. Just a lone sagebrush shaded by a massive saguaro. A rabbit hopped away, darting in between bushes and trees until Jamis lost sight of it. A gecko ran across the wall, racetrack fast.

The sun dipped and was gone in a blink and the air chilled instantly. Jamis lit the ground with her phone flashlight. It was just dirt. Jamis turned off the light and turned in circles, trying to ascertain the source of her hunch and unease. The light inside the RV glowed warm orange. Sapphire's shadow was visible in the kitchen bench.

Something moved on the backside of the property, where Charlie pointed to the orange flag. It was a man wearing a baseball hat. They stared at each other. Twilight was not complete yet, and the few remaining moments of dusk allowed Jamis to be certain what she saw. It wasn't a ghost. It was a real live human male and they were in the middle of nowhere.

Something about him triggered her sense of impending danger. She'd learned how to sense predatory men from early adolescence, the awful reality of her early life's poverty and later, in foster care. She'd paid a terrible price for the sense, but it had kept her safe since she was old enough to assert her own boundaries. Males like this vibrated with a different frequency.

There was a flash of light and when Jamis finished blinking, he was gone, obscured by growing twilight.

Sapphire was alone in the trailer. Jamis reacted from instinct and broke out into a sprint.

"Sapphire," Jamis screamed, in route. "Sapphire," she called again, bounding up the metal stairs. "Get off the phone." Jamis slammed the door shut and fumbled with the locks. "There's someone out there. Call Carmen. Hurry."

"Oh my God, Sam, I'll call you back," Sapphire said. She dialed Carmen. "You gotta come back. There is someone here." Jamis couldn't hear Carmen on the other end. "Well, I don't know."

"A real live human man and he was over by the weird room," Jamis said.

"What room? I don't understand," Sapphire said, panicked.

"The room with the orange flag thingy. That Charlie said we couldn't go in," Jamis explained.

"Did you hear Jamis?" Sapphire asked Carmen. "Yeah, I don't know. Call nine-one-one," Sapphire said and hung up.

A sharp bang against the back window of the RV shook the trailer. Someone was banging on the window. He hit it hard, but the glass didn't break. Jamis touched the window near her. It was a sort of refined plexiglass. She opened the kitchen drawers looking for weapons and found two steak knives. She handed one to Sapphire who was frantically dialing 9-1-1 on the phone.

"I lost the signal. It's not working. Let's hope Carmen can get through," she told Jamis, voice quivery. The pounding continued, down the side of the RV. Jamis pulled Sapphire to the other end and turned off the lights. The pounding stopped. There was only the vague outline of the man through the far window.

"What should we do?" Jamis spoke but didn't expect an answer.

"Is he a ghost?" Sapphire watched the figure walk around the RV, movements slow and methodical.

"No. I wouldn't be so afraid if he were dead. Living humans scare the shit out of me. Generally, they do the most damage," Jamis said.

Jamis crept up by the far window and peered out. He was walking toward the house. His pace was even, and he moved with eerie confidence. He disappeared into the house, only to return a few moments later.

"Holy hell, he's got a freaking ax," Jamis said, voice low.

"Okay. This is a bad situation. But we're smart women. I mean, really smart. We need to focus," Sapphire said.

"Yeah, okay, so he's going to chop into one side of this thing so we have to be ready to run to the other side and get out. Once we do, should we split up or stay together?" Jamis asked as he moved closer.

"Together. You've got the car keys. Unlock the car as soon as we get out the door. We both run in that direction," Sapphire said.

"Take the keys and go ahead of me. I'm stronger, I think. No offense," Jamis said.

"None taken," Sapphire said, obviously agreeing.

"If I go down, you run over him with the car, okay?"

Sapphire took the keys. The ax split the plexiglass window in two at the rear end of the RV. They pushed open the door and ran. The moon was dull and barely a sliver. It was so dark. Jamis saw nothing until Sapphire unlocked the car with the remote. Headlights flashed and cut through the night. There were footsteps behind them. Labored breathing. She didn't want to turn around. Sapphire made it to the driver's side of the car when something tripped Jamis.

She struggled to stand, but something was wrapped around her legs. Its grip tightened into a painful squeeze. Sapphire turned on the headlights.

It was the demon from earlier, grinning at her again, eyes maniacal. "Going somewhere?"

Jamis kicked her legs. The man was closing in. There was nowhere to go and nothing to do. Without options, she punched the demon. It screamed and unfurled, disappearing in a spurt of red and yellow vapors. Jamis scrambled to her feet, ready to meet her fate head-on when Sapphire gunned the engine of the car. Her intention was clear and their assailant saw it. He stopped running toward Jamis and looked at the car, then back at her.

"Think you can make it?" Jamis asked, now on her feet and angry.

"Maybe I wanna try," he said.

"Who the hell are you? I mean, if you were shocked to find us here, knock politely. Was all this really necessary?"

"You always this wise-ass?" He took a few steps toward her, ax head dragging on the ground.

"Are you always this cliché 'I'm a 1980s slasher movie, ax wielding maniac, terrorizing women under starlight' or is this special for me?" Jamis asked. She'd not let go of the steak knife and almost laughed at the image of her dueling with it while he wielded the ax.

"You don't know what you're getting into, but it's best if you left it alone," he said.

"Stop walking or I'll have her run you over," Jamis said. He paused. The angles were in their favor. Jamis held up her hand to Sapphire.

"Listen, I just came out here hunting ghosts," Jamis said to him.

"I know who you are. She told me," the man said.

"Always nice to meet a fan," Jamis said.

"Well, I guess we're in a standoff," he said.

"Maybe," Jamis said.

The man turned his head to the side, like he was whispering to someone.

"You always talk to yourself?" Jamis waved the steak knife in the air. For some reason, it made her feel better. Open, hostile defiance was her earliest coping mechanism and still her best.

"I'm not supposed to be doing this," he said.

In the distance, she heard sirens. "Yeah. Listen. I don't think those are coming to help you."

"Yeah, well, since you had to stick your nose in it, know what happens next is on you. You're lucky she doesn't want you dead," he said. Then he turned and ran the other way. Sapphire gunned the car forward and Jamis hopped in.

"Follow him," Jamis said. Sapphire complied. They circled around the back of the house and came to a skidding halt at the barbwire. He jumped it and disappeared. He'd likely parked his vehicle somewhere in the area. The desert was so dark they'd never find him.

Jamis locked the car doors, just to be sure.

"What the he—" but her words were cut off. Behind them, an explosion rocked the car. Heat swarmed them like bees. Jamis felt it sting her skin.

"Drive, drive," Jamis yelled. Sapphire did. The screeching of the barbwire against the metal of the car joined the roar behind them. The initial propulsion of gas carried them farther into the desert. Once the car stopped moving, they turned in their seats to look. The house was in flames. There was a crater where the orange flag had flown. Cop cars careened toward them. They glimpsed sirens through dancing flames.

"Do you blow everything up and set it on fire?" Sapphire asked.

"I have a style," Jamis said. Sapphire put her head on the steering wheel. "I once set a mattress on fire in a hotel room."

The back of their rental car was charred and the tires were melted. They left it where it was in the desert on the other side of the barbwire and cautiously approached the cops, waving their arms. They needed to escape the heat of the blast. In a tense moment, a few officers had jumped from their cars guns out.

"Sherriff's office. Put your hands up where I can see them," an officer yelled.

"Don't shoot. Don't shoot. We're not the bad guys," Jamis yelled back.

"Put your hands up and stop moving," he yelled again.

"I really need to clear this heat. Let me just approach. I'm not armed," Jamis said.

"Stop moving," he yelled.

"I can't because we will literally burn up," Jamis said.

"I will shoot," he said.

"And I will sue you," Jamis yelled back. Sapphire grabbed her arm.

"Just stop," she said. They stopped. The officer pulled them forward by their arms.

"Don't you grab me like that," Jamis said, fighting the officer. "I did nothing wrong. You don't even know what's happened and you're treating me like a criminal." Indignation burned inside her.

"Shut up," the officer said. Jamis yanked away from him.

"Seriously, I have a lot of money to spend on legal fees. Now don't touch me or her again." Jamis grabbed Sapphire by the arm and darted past the officer.

"That's enough," someone said. It was another officer in a different color uniform. "Let them be. We got a call that two women were out here at risk of assault."

"Thank you," Jamis said.

"What happened?" The reasonable officer approached her.

"No idea. This guy just showed up. He was over six foot tall. Thin. Creepy vibe. We spotted each other," Jamis told him. She relayed the details of the encounter and when finished, asked Sapphire, "Miss anything?"

Sapphire shook her head. There was black soot on her face.

"So he chased you, you got to the car, followed him, and then this happened," the officer said.

"Pretty much. It was quite a blast," Sapphire said.

"Pun intended," Jamis said and Sapphire laughed.

"Okay, just don't go anywhere. We've got paramedics on the way, and they will check you out," the officer said.

"We gotta make sure this fire stays contained," another officer said in the distance. Jamis's legs felt wobbly, her heart hammered. She grabbed Sapphire's hand and pulled her away from the chaos.

What the hell had they walked into?

For the most part, the fire had died down. The explosion was centralized in the weird pit with torture devices Jamis never got to see. Firefighters, paramedics, and cops swarmed the property. Jamis and Sapphire sat in the open back doors of an ambulance. Neither one of them were hurt or needed care. There just wasn't anywhere else to sit.

At some point, Carmen arrived with Gwen and Charlie, but Jamis lost all track of time. Carmen leaned nonchalantly against the ambulance's open door. Charlie and Gwen were talking with cops. The house and RV were blackened and smoldering. They'd likely have to just tear everything down and sell the land. Jamis felt a twinge of guilt but then remembered they'd reached out to her. Sapphire had called Sam, and now as the dust settled, Jamis wanted to hear Johnna's voice. But as she began to dial, the officer who threatened to shoot her approached.

"I don't believe any of this. There was no one else out here," he said.

"I don't want to talk to you," Jamis said.

"It doesn't add up. None of it. Why did you plant that bomb? For attention? Publicity?"

Jamis didn't respond. Deep fatigue settled into her bones. How many altercations could one person survive? Was she subconsciously manifesting deep unease? Is that why she constantly found herself in these situations? The man in front of her blazed with anger. What issue did he have with her? Did she trigger some deep-seated emotion? Look like his first girlfriend, ex-wife, or estranged sister? Jamis knew she wasn't everyone's taste. She had rough edges and enough attitude to make her difficult in the best of circumstances. But this level of disdain was ridiculous. They were the victims, after all.

"Answer me," the officer said.

"Not without a lawyer," Jamis said, resolved.

"And not without another officer present," Sapphire said, shifting closer to Jamis.

"It would be best if you dialed it down," Carmen said.

"Dial it down?" He put his hand on his gun.

"You feel like a tough guy with that gun, but it's all pretense. You're probably secretly longing for your mommy, so you know, strong women make you uncomfortable," Jamis said.

He grabbed her by the wrist, yanked her forward, and had handcuffs on her before anyone knew what happened. Jamis was stunned. Her phone was forgotten in the dirt. Carmen yelled and Sapphire grabbed her arm. He shoved Jamis in the back of a car.

"Call her lawyer, because she needs one," he said. Jamis kicked at the door of the car but it wouldn't budge. There were no handles. A barrier separated her and the cop. He slammed the car door, started the engine, and raced from the site.

"What the hell?" Jamis asked. She adjusted her posture in the back seat and began kicking at the metal cage separating them.

"Stop it or I'll shoot you," he said.

"You can't do this," Jamis said, kicking harder.

"I did," he said.

"I have rights. I didn't do anything. You can't just arrest people," Jamis said.

"She's been waiting for you. This is just my part," he said.

Deep, sick dread spread through Jamis like a spilled oil tanker in water. It was slimy and it invaded every crevice of her body. She stopped kicking and sat up.

"Who is she?" There was nothing to do. Her hands were cinched painfully behind her back. The police car was locked up tight.

"You know her," he said, meeting her eyes in the rearview mirror.

"No, I really don't," Jamis said.

"She told me to take you. I just heard her on our way out here. I couldn't say no."

"You didn't know her before?" Jamis leaned forward on the seat. He was driving way too fast on the dirt road. The speedometer read seventy-five. The car bounced uncomfortably. If he hit a pothole, it might pop the tire and it was her best chance of surviving.

"No," he said. Hesitation flashed in his eyes. Jamis saw and seized it. It was better than a pothole.

"You don't want to do this. I won't file a complaint. This will ruin your life," Jamis said. He let up on the pedal. Jamis pressed. "Some evil entity is using you to interact with the physical world. I didn't think it was actually possible, but it seems to be. I don't think you're a bad guy. I don't want you to be hurt by this, but I need you to stop, get out of the car, let me go."

His hands tightened on the wheel. His jaw clenched. The car slowed more. Sweat rolled down his face.

"I think you were the first person on scene." Jamis waited.

"I wasn't though," he said. He took one hand off the wheel and rubbed his face. "I don't know what happened."

"Well, whatever is there, on that property, seized control of you somehow. I don't know how. I have to rethink everything I know about demonic possession after tonight."

The car hit a hole, but they kept going, now about forty-five. "What's your name?" Jamis decided a personal connection was the best bet.

"Levi," he said through gritted teeth. His voice was different, not so deep. Veins on his neck bulged. He wiped his forehead with his arm and gripped the wheel again.

"Levi, what's your last name?"

"Martinez," he said.

"Let's stop the car and get out and talk," Jamis said. There were car lights on I-10.

"I don't know that I can," Levi said.

"You can. Let's stop right up there before the freeway," Jamis said.

"I'm supposed to take you to Jerome."

"That's a bit of a drive so late. I'm kind of tired. Long day," Jamis said. Levi let up off the gas again. They slowed to thirty-five. "You married?"

"No, but I've got a girlfriend."

"What's her name?" Their speed dropped to twenty-five.

"Alice," Levi said.

"Let's pull over and call her," Jamis said.

He let off the gas and they drifted to the side of the road, right before the entrance ramp to I-10. Semis and cars whooshed by. Levi put his head on the steering wheel and cried.

Jamis let him, for a few minutes, until she couldn't take her arms being bound any longer. "Levi, I need you to let me out." His eyes opened.

"Shit," he said. He jumped from the car, opened the back door, and pulled Jamis out. He undid her handcuffs. "I'm so sorry. What happened?"

"You don't remember?"

"It's like a dream I had, but it's fading, like they do when you first wake up."

Jamis took a few steps back from him and shook out her arms. It reminded her of being bound in the spring, in the front room of Stephanie's home. None of it was pleasant reminiscence. In the distance, sirens approached them.

"I think something possessed you," Jamis said.

"What?"

"Yeah. I saw a demon there. Something got in you, or commandeered you, or just exerted influence on you," Jamis said.

"To Jerome," Levi said.

The sirens were closer. Her friends must have convinced them to come after her. "Why Jerome?"

He wiped his eyes, looked at the approaching cars. "I just kept seeing this place. And a mine, maybe? Big steel equipment. I knew right where to go."

"Where?" Jamis pressed him, wanting answers before the cops got to them.

"I mean, I can see it but I don't know it. I could take you there, but I don't know how to describe it," Levi said. He looked young and vulnerable.

"Yeah," Jamis said, turning to look at the cops. "I need you to."

"I'm going to be in so much trouble," Levi said.

"I'll try to help," Jamis said.

"How?"

"I mean, you were possessed. I'll tell them that," Jamis said, her tone telling him the answer was obvious.

"Maybe helping me isn't the best course of action. It sounds crazy now," Levi said.

"Story of my life," Jamis said.

CHAPTER SIX

There was a great deal of haggling about jurisdiction, but eventually, Arizona Highway Patrol prevailed, and Jamis was picked up off the side of the road and driven into Phoenix. She didn't know what had happened to Levi but hoped he was okay.

Sapphire and Carmen were ushered into town in a cruiser behind her. Sapphire managed to pass her phone to her before they were separated. Jamis called Johnna from the back seat of the cruiser and tried to calmly explain what happened. By the end of the phone call, Johnna thought she should come to Phoenix, if for no other reason than to make sure Jamis was released from police custody. Jamis made her promise not to rush to Arizona and reassured her that she'd call as soon as possible.

It had been two hours since that call, and her clothes were filthy and smelled like smoke. Sapphire still had soot smeared across her face. They sat side by side in a small office in the highway patrol field office, where they had just finished telling them everything that happened.

"Are they ever going to let us out?" Sapphire rested her head on her arms.

"Let's just leave. I've been patient enough," Jamis said. She stood, yanked open the door, and Sapphire followed.

"I was just coming in to tell you we can take you to a hotel," an officer said. "We appreciate your help and would like to ask you not leave town."

"Yeah," Jamis said, fatigued and tired. She missed Johnna and Virginia and wanted to go home. "All our luggage is in the desert," Jamis said.

"Shit," Sapphire said and leaned against her.

"Do you want—" the officer began to say, but Jamis cut him off.

"No, it's fine. A hotel would be awesome."

They followed him through the building and waved to Carmen waiting in the lobby. She was on her feet and to them almost immediately. "You okay? You hurt?"

Jamis shook her head and moped outside. It took a lot of effort to get into the car. Sapphire looked like she was in similar shape. Jamis's nerves were so frayed the car door shutting made her flinch. She closed her eyes and leaned her head against the window.

"Where to?" It was the officer.

"Anywhere with a bed," Sapphire said.

"I'll take you to a Holiday Inn, right around the corner," he said, and Sapphire gave him a thumbs-up.

"Our stuff is in the back of the rental car. Oh my God, the rental car. I have to deal with that too," Jamis said.

"We towed it into town for you. I'll give you the address," the officer said.

"So our stuff is there," Sapphire said. She turned to Carmen. "Do you have your stuff?"

"Yeah. I had it with me," Carmen said.

"But who was the guy out there? And why did he try to kill us with an ax? And why did he blow up the hole? And who is the 'she' they keep telling me about?" Jamis rubbed her eyes with her hand. They burned and she needed eye drops.

"Don't start. Let's sleep and regroup in the morning," Sapphire said, hands up.

But their highway patrol officer had a different idea. "Yeah, that's what we don't get. But right before we left, a couple of detectives from Phoenix PD showed up to look at our notes. They wanted your information so they might contact you."

"Why would Phoenix police be concerned with something that happened near Blythe?" Carmen turned to him as she asked the question, clearly tired as well.

"That's what we wondered, but they said there was a similar situation about three weeks ago, toward Tucson, out on the other side of the reservations and they've somehow tied it to a larger case they're investigating."

"What larger case?" Jamis was alert again.

"No idea," the officer said, but something in his tone suggested he knew more than he said. He put the car in park. "Here we are. Just be careful."

The gold yellow light from the Holiday Inn sign illuminated his face, which was hardened, but his eyes were kind. Jamis touched his shoulder, thanking him with a nod, and they climbed from the car. The temperature was perfect and air still. Jamis booked them each a room and they split up into their own silent spaces.

"Lock your door," Jamis said to them both. They waved, acknowledging her, and she watched them disappear into their rooms.

Inside her room, Jamis stripped and climbed into the shower and scrubbed the soot from her body and washed her hair multiple times.

She FaceTimed Johnna, wrapped in a towel. Johnna answered after one ring. She was in the bedroom, lights on. Virginia was curled up behind her, head on her hip. Jamis's whole body sighed when she saw her. Her red-blond hair was pulled back and up on her head. She wore a tank top and light green yoga pants.

"Jamis, what happened?" She told her, up to the conversation with the highway patrol officer, just a few minutes before. Johnna listened, not interrupting, and then said, "I should not have encouraged this."

"No, it's not your fault," Jamis said.

"Can you walk away? Just come home tomorrow," Johnna said.

"I'm already thinking about it. But then what's next? What do I do if I don't chase ghosts?"

"Anything you want. I'm sure you can find something," Johnna said, tone softer. Then, after a few moments, "A demon, Jamis?"

"I mean, I don't even know about this demon thingy. But don't forget the possessed cop, the wafty black smoky thing, the dude with the ax, or what's even in Jerome," Jamis said.

"It's asking for trouble," Johnna said.

"It really is," Jamis said, turning on her other side. "I feel like maybe some of my eyelashes got burned off in the blast."

"Really? Hold the phone closer," Johnna said with a smile. Jamis grinned at her, heart expanding. The hotel room was sterile and quiet. She'd slept in so many and never noticed how empty they were before she stayed at Johnna's home. Now, it felt like the first home she'd had since her mom died. Life changed in seconds, with illness, injury, and death. Jamis knew she was a finite creature, balanced on the edge of oblivion like every other being on the planet. She wasn't convinced there was any meaning to anything at all. Just experience. Growth. Change. And inevitable decay. Despite all that, she'd lived the hero's journey, demanding that there was truth to be found, questions worth asking, and hope that one day she'd understand why she was alive at all. Johnna did a lot to answer that question for her.

"I'll think about coming home," Jamis said.

"Good," Johnna said and touched the phone screen. "I miss you. No demons."

"None. I promise," Jamis said.

"You need to sleep," Johnna said.

"You too." Jamis closed her eyes. "Let's just fall to sleep on FaceTime together, okay?"

"I love you. Good dreams only," Johnna said.

Sleep was already settling over Jamis. But she said, right before darkness enveloped her, "I love you, too."

❖

Jamis was on a plateau. Sharp, red mountains jutted from the ground in front of her. There was a pit in the ground from a ceased mining operation. The wind blew and a heavy fog blanketed the horizon. Jamis looked over her shoulder. It was Jerome, balanced on the sides of a mountain, houses and buildings on stilts. Jerome made her anxious because she thought it was likely to fall apart at any moment.

There was a sound in the distance. It was grating, like a steel blade scraped repeatedly against a sharpening block. It was the same sound she heard in the desert during the day. Then there was a shout, followed by a scream. Jamis rushed toward the sounds, her instinct to help. The hill was steep and her legs burned. She fell, climbing on hands and knees, clawing her way to the top. The knees of her jeans tore and sharp rocks dug into her skin. At the top, Jamis found her balance and wiped dirt from her pants.

Dark clouds rolled across the sky. A carriage bounded by her, pulled by a horse, and she screamed, rushing off the road. It kicked dust up behind it and she covered her mouth with her forearm, trying to avoid inhalation. Somewhere, a bell rung and with it, throngs of men filled the street, clothes filthy, faces black with dirt. The smell was overpowering.

Then, there was a woman. The crowds split apart as she walked toward Jamis. Her dress was black. Her eyes bright blue. She felt familiar, but Jamis couldn't place her. The woman stopped and then men all around her disappeared. Just evaporated. The clouds disappeared and the sun blazed. It burned Jamis's skin and she moved her arm from her mouth to her eyes.

She was dreaming. It was a dream. She was in a hotel room where she'd just FaceTimed Johnna.

Jamis took her arm off her eyes and breathed into the experience. She didn't need to react with fear. None of it was real. But it was interesting, and she didn't want to wake up.

She took a few long strides toward the woman. The dream allowed her. As she walked, the streets of Jerome changed with her. The dirt turned to asphalt and the wooden building next to her into brick. The horse drawn carriages changed to cars. But the town was empty. There was no life Jamis could sense.

"Hello," the woman said.

"Are you the 'she' everyone keeps telling me about?"

"That's not a nice greeting," she said.

"Well, it just felt like I was on fire, so I'm not in a good mood," Jamis said.

"I just wanted your attention," the woman said.

"Well, I guess you got it," Jamis said.

"No, I've been trying to get it for a long time." Her face faded in and out of view. This wasn't like talking with Emma. This felt different. This woman hadn't come to her for help. She had something else in mind.

"You're wondering why you're here," the woman said.

"Yeah," Jamis said, but nothing else. Suddenly, she was overcome with a desire to get far away. Something about the woman terrified her.

"I was hoping your young friend would bring you to me," the woman said.

"My young friend?" Jamis tried to bring awareness to her sleeping self, urge her body to move and wake from what was happening. Her terror now outweighed her curiosity.

"Yes, whom you so kindly talked into stopping the car," she said.

The cop, Levi. "Yeah, well, he was busy already. Had plans and a life," Jamis said.

The woman laughed, and when her mouth opened, there was nothing inside her. Just dark, open space. Her mouth opened wider, showing the black hole inside, and then folded backward, consuming the woman, until they blinked out of existence. Jamis was alone in the street, standing in front of a shop. Her heart rate was high, breathing shallow. She had to wake up.

But then the ground under her feet shook and she heard more shouts. She raced back down the hill and looked over the cliff. Large, heavy equipment moved across the ground, scraping copper from the hills.

A man ran toward her, shouting for help. The woman she'd just met chased him, and before Jamis could get to him, he was swallowed. Somehow the woman's essence consumed him. The woman waved and blinked away. She'd seen this before.

This moment had happened before.

Jamis stepped, and with it, she was in the lobby of a hotel. Maggie waited by the stairs. "Well, are you coming?" She gestured impatiently at Jamis.

"Go ahead. I'm not with you anymore," Jamis said. Maggie disappeared and Jamis made her way down the long hallway. There was a picture at the end, but a huge hole in the floor kept her from it. She backed up, her intention to run and jump across the hole, but when she did, she fell through darkness, like she was dropping from a skyscraper. She screamed, legs flailing, and just before the bottom came, she woke.

Jamis sat up in bed. Her phone was off. Bright light filtered into the room through cracks in the blinds. A man stood at the end of her bed.

"She's coming for you," he said and disappeared. Jamis leapt from the bed and threw open the blinds.

The clock on her phone said it was five thirty in the morning. She'd slept for two hours and didn't feel like her eyes closed.

CHAPTER SEVEN

Once the man was gone, Jamis fell onto to the bed, spread across it, long arms and legs draped over the sides. The stakes were higher than they'd ever been for her. She'd not just encountered demonic, poltergeist activity at the house the night before. She'd also come face-to-face with another very scary alive human. She rubbed her eyes with her hands.

"What is going on?" She spoke to herself and the empty room. Maybe she should just pack it up and return to Johnna, let it go. Letting go was always a choice, though she was terrible at doing it. She should just go back to sleep, but she needed to find the rental car, get her bags, and put on clean clothes as a matter of priority. It felt more important than sleep.

But her legs were too tired to stand, so she shifted on the bed and shut her eyes for a while longer. Sleep came faster than her conscious mind had supposed it would, and she fell into imageless slumber. Knocking on the door woke her a few hours later.

Sapphire wore the same dirty clothes from the night before. Jamis was in a towel.

"Oh God," Sapphire said, hand over her eyes. "Put your clothes on. I'll Uber us a ride to our luggage and another rental car. Then we'll get Carmen."

Jamis shut the door without answering. Her mouth tasted awful so she tried to scrub it clean with a small bottle of Listerine. She cringed as she pulled on her dirty clothes and left the socks in the trash. It only took a few minutes.

When she opened the door, Sapphire was still in the hallway. "Ready?"

"Yeah," Jamis said.

"Thanks for not being naked in your towel," Sapphire said. They walked quietly down the hall together, slumped and tired.

"I had a crazy dream," Jamis said.

"Please no," Sapphire said.

"Yeah. It was in Jerome," Jamis said.

"Is this like last time?"

"I think so. I think it's like with Emma but different. I'll tell you about it in the car," Jamis said. She detoured for a cup of complimentary coffee. Sapphire filled two cups. "Double fisting it."

"I'm so tired," Sapphire said.

They climbed into their Uber, a beat-up black Hyundai, and Jamis stared out the window while Sapphire gave the addresses for the destinations. Their first stop was to get luggage, and the next, to get their own rental car. Jamis drifted through it, half-awake, preoccupied by the dream she described to Sapphire in exacting detail. Johnna called as she was signing the paperwork for the rental car, but she asked to return her call in a minute.

By the time they arrived back to the hotel, Jamis was convinced she needed to go to Jerome. Sapphire reluctantly agreed but told Jamis if anyone else tried to kill her, or anything else blew up, she was on the next plane home.

Sapphire waved to her over her shoulder and shut her hotel room door behind her. Jamis knocked on Carmen's door. Her small travel bag was somehow mixed in with theirs and she wanted her to have whatever was in it.

Carmen answered, bleary-eyed. "We got our bags. I'm going to shower, again, and get dressed. Then I think we should get some food. Want to go?"

"Come get me when you're ready," Carmen said and shut the door.

In her own room, Jamis scrubbed clean and dressed in clean clothes. Her toothbrush felt like a miracle. The toothpaste was nectar from heaven. During her childhood, as a ward of the State of California, Jamis learned to savor simple privileges. Clean clothes, hygiene products, and a safe room to rest were her deepest desires. To get them, she did nothing but study and read. It was her way out of poverty.

Maybe it was because of all this that the chaos of the night before triggered a deeper resolve in her. She would persevere. She'd not called Johnna back yet. But when she did, Johnna might be upset to hear that her determination, which bordered on obsession, had won out against cautious consideration. She hoped not, but Jamis had to see this out now.

A very bad woman hijacked her dreams. A demon terrorized her. A scary man chased Sapphire and her with an ax. A man infiltrated her hotel room.

There was no running from what was to come. Her only option was to square to it, look it in the eye, and see it through. Jamis knew no other way to live.

Jamis sat next to Carmen in the booth. They decided to eat at the hotel restaurant.

"This is nothing like Tess's food back home," Jamis said.

"Back home. Our colloquialisms might be wearing off on you," Sapphire said.

"Yeah, she's proper town folk," Carmen said.

Jamis pushed her egg around her plate. It was runny and gooey and undercooked. Sapphire and Carmen ate pancakes that looked like cardboard. Jamis picked at her hash browns, preoccupied with how she'd tell Johnna she wasn't coming home until she sorted out her new poltergeist.

The blinds on the window next to them were turned downward to block out the sun, but the parking lot was still visible. A young man stood by the front door, hand to his eyes. Jamis watched him for a few moments before she realized it was Levi.

"I'll be right back," she said and left the table abruptly. She pushed through the front doors of the restaurant and called out to him. He turned to the sound of his name and moved hurriedly to her.

"Hi." He stopped in front of her, arms crossed on his chest. His dark brown eyes were bloodshot and red-rimmed. His hair was disheveled, and a dark shadow of beard was visible on his cheeks.

"You look rough," Jamis said.

"I feel rough. I'm suspended, pending review. My girlfriend kicked me out. She said she'd given me too many tries to get my life together. Do you know how hard someone like me had to work to get a job on the police force? I honestly don't know what I'm going to do. My mom told me I'm a disgrace. Wouldn't let me in her house."

"I'm so sorry. But how did you find me?"

"A friend with patrol knew where you were staying," he said, wiping a tear from his cheek. "It's not your fault. But man, what happened out there? When I tried to sleep like two hours ago, in the back seat of my truck, my dreams showed me you. We were in Jerome and this crazy, evil lady ate a guy."

"What the hell," Jamis said. It happened in her dream too. "Come sit and eat with us." The heat was too much to handle with everything else she was carrying.

He followed her dutifully. Back at the booth, Jamis sat next to Carmen and waved for Levi to join. He slid in next to Sapphire, who upon seeing him, shouted. "Oh, hell no."

"It's okay. He got possessed or something," Jamis said.

"Yeah, I was possessed," Levi said to Sapphire.

"That's what they always say. Oh, I was consumed by my testosterone. Oh, I had shareholders to answer to, so I had to fire laborers. Oh, I had to pay myself a massive bonus from taxpayer bailouts while evicting people from their homes. It's the history of patriarchal capitalism," Sapphire said.

"How did this end up in political theory?" Jamis sipped her coffee.

"Everything ends up in political theory," Sapphire said.

"He stopped the car, remember?" Jamis stared at Sapphire.

"He could be playing you. It could be part of the plan. When they realized they couldn't get you to Jerome last night, this was the new approach," Sapphire said.

"That's fair," Jamis said.

"It's not fair," Levi said.

"I don't care if you think it's fair. The last time I saw you, Jamis ended up manhandled into the back of a squad car, kidnapped," Sapphire said.

"Okay, if I may," Carmen interrupted.

"Please," Jamis said.

"Why are you here?" Carmen stared at Levi. Her gaze was direct and commanding.

"Well, ma'am, I feel bad about what happened. I got suspended and my girlfriend broke up with me in the middle of the night, and my mom said I couldn't move in, and I thought maybe if I found Jamis, I could fix it. I had dreams," he said, stuttering and nervous.

"Ma'am," Jamis said. Carmen ignored her.

"What do you think should happen now?" Sapphire turned so her back was against the wall, as much distance between herself and Levi as possible.

"I want to take Jamis to Jerome and show her what I saw in my head last night," Levi said.

"Let's go," Jamis said.

"Whoa. Not yet. The officer told us to stick around for a bit," Sapphire said.

"We're just going to Jerome," Jamis said.

"What's in Jerome?" It was Carmen who asked this, tone still even.

"I don't know. But I'll know it when I see it. I've never actually been there," Levi said.

"I have. Long time ago. I saw something there I saw in my dream last night. It's all connected. I've got to go to Jerome," Jamis said. This was the only logical next step. She had to pursue the visions her new poltergeist was giving her. "Let's finish eating, go by the field office where we were last night, see what else is going on, and then head up."

"I'm going to regret this," Sapphire said.

"You always say that," Jamis said.

"There is no talking you out of this, is there?" Johnna picked up her return phone call on the first ring.

"It's not even about talking me out of it or not. It's more like it's something I feel must be done," Jamis said.

"I understand. Just be careful. Keep me updated," Johnna said. Jamis breathed through a ton of worry into relief. She anticipated an ultimatum or disappointment. But Johnna wouldn't do that, and she should have known better. Unlike her, Johnna could let go and allow.

"God, I'm so relieved you're not pissed," Jamis said.

"Pissed? No. Anxious and worried, yes. But I trust you'll be okay. You survived how many years before me?"

"I'm not really sure how I did that," Jamis said and Johnna didn't speak but Jamis was sure she smiled.

"I love you," Johnna said.

"You too," Jamis said and she released the phone call and waved to Levi who strode across the parking lot to her.

Sapphire and Carmen followed behind. Sapphire watched Levi like he was a serial killer waiting for the right moment to slaughter them.

"Follow us to the patrol office. I'll run in. See what's going on," Jamis said. He agreed.

Jamis tossed Carmen the car keys and crawled into the back seat. She was bone weary and couldn't face driving. Sapphire plugged the address in the GPS and set out, in silence. They navigated unfamiliar streets to the highway patrol field office, found a parking spot, and Jamis asked them to wait for her. She strode across the parking lot like she owned the place and pushed into the lobby. For a confused moment, Jamis thought she was back in Sage Creek, looking for Detective Daniels.

Instead, a woman greeted her from behind a wall of thick bulletproof glass. "You need something?"

"I was here last night. An explosion out toward Blythe."

"Oh, yeah, you," the woman said.

"Right. I need to talk to someone about it. They told me to stay in town, but I've gotta go to Jerome," Jamis said.

"Hold on," the woman said. She punched buttons on a phone.

Jamis rested her arms against the counter. The woman hung up and pointed. A door opened. It was the officer from the night before.

"Hi," he said.

"You're still here?"

"Pulling a double," he said.

"I'm heading up to Jerome for the day," Jamis said.

"The Phoenix cops took off earlier, but they have your contact info so if they call, just answer," he said.

"It's all good then? You won't issue an APB for me?"

"Well, while we'd all like to know what happened out there last night, we don't actually think you had anything to do with it. Somehow you were just there," he said.

"Happens a lot," Jamis said.

"My wife likes you," he said, smiling.

"Send her my best, and thanks," Jamis said. He turned and left her with a wave.

Outside, she walked to Levi's truck. At his driver's side window, she told him, "Okay, follow us. When we get closer, you take the lead and take me where you were supposed to."

"You want to ride with me?"

"Are you kidding me?" Jamis was shocked at the question.

"I'm just kind of emotional and lonely," he said.

"Embrace it. That shit is transformational. If it turns out you're not a serial killer, maniac, or just general jerk, I'll help you find a therapist. Maybe even a job," Jamis said.

She opened the back door of the car and climbed back in. "We're a go."

Sapphire set the GPS for Jerome.

CHAPTER EIGHT

It was about two and a half hours to Jerome. When they stopped to eat and rest at a McDonald's just off I-17 before the AZ-260 cutover to Jerome, Carmen handed Jamis the keys.

"But I'm tired," Jamis said.

"Me too," Carmen said.

"I'll drive," Sapphire said and took the keys.

Levi waved at Jamis.

"Hey, doing okay?" Jamis tucked her hands in her pockets to brace against a grating wind that made the heat worse. It came from every direction, relentless and hard. This high desert felt nothing like Sage Creek.

"Yeah, I just feel like you should ride with me now," Levi said. He rubbed his eyes and took a long sip of soda. He held a bag of food. "You can even drive if you want."

"Why do you want me to ride with you?"

"It's just I'm kind of scared and I feel really sad," he said.

For some odd reason, Jamis felt responsible for him. Maybe because he'd lost everything being possessed by a demon trying to get her to Jerome. Or maybe the lost look on his young face reminded Jamis of her younger self, unsure, unloved, and adrift. Instinctually, she knew there was nothing to fear from Levi. If anything, the only thing she needed to worry about was that he might imprint on her like a baby duck and never stop following her.

"Okay, okay. If we can convince Sapphire," she said. He smiled and there was relief evident in it. Just then, Sapphire arrived at her side. "I'm riding with Levi," Jamis told her, bracing for pushback.

"You know, if you get chopped up into tiny pieces by a serial killer, I'm the one who will have to comfort Johnna," Sapphire said.

"I'm not a serial killer," Levi said. Sapphire stared at him. "I swear. I'm really sad, actually."

"His feelings are hurt because his girlfriend kicked him out and his mom won't let him move back in," Jamis said.

"Why are we taking Levi to Jerome? Remind me again," Sapphire said.

"He had the same dream as me. There's a spot we have to go," Jamis said.

Sapphire leaned toward Levi. "If you hurt her, I will ruin your life. I will ruin the life of everyone you know and care about."

"I mean, she can do it," Jamis said. Levi looked at Jamis, startled. "She's a computer genius."

"It's true," Sapphire said.

"I won't," Levi said and scooted away from her. He climbed over the console and buckled himself into the passenger side. Jamis got in and adjusted the seat.

"Follow me," she said to Sapphire who stalked back to the car. They left the parking lot and turned onto the road to Jerome, navigating winding roads that opened up to expansive, flat desert. It was not the haunting emptiness of the desert toward California. It was populated by small towns, businesses, franchises, and gas stations. Jamis kept to the speed limit.

"I don't know what's happening," Levi said.

"It's pretty much always like this for me," Jamis said.

"I think that I'm supposed to take you to a place that overlooks Jerome," Levi said.

"Probably not totally comfortable with that proposition," Jamis said.

"It's like I see the place but I've never been, so I don't know what it is. I've seen pictures of the Grand Hotel up there, and it looks like that, up high, but it's not."

"Well, we're just about twenty minutes out or so," Jamis said.

"Soon enough, I guess," Levi said, chin in his hand, staring out the window. Jamis glanced in the rearview mirror. Sapphire and Carmen were still behind her.

They turned on the road that would take them into Jerome and Jamis slowed her breath. It wound like a snake, the truck hugging the side of the road as it climbed up the mountain. There was curve after curve. Jamis lost count.

"Holy shit," Levi said.

"It's a shock after being in the flat infrastructure of Phoenix," Jamis said.

"It's a shock after being anywhere," Levi said.

Finally, the road delivered them to Cleopatra Hill, the mountain Jerome was built upon. But still they climbed, the roads narrow, the scenic view breathtaking but terrifying. Jamis parked the car in open parking in the middle of the main street, next to a scenic view, and got out. Levi followed. Sapphire parked next to her.

"That was jacked up," Sapphire told her.

"You two never been off-roading at home?" Carmen said, smiling. She walked to the edge to study the scenery. It made Jamis nervous. "I think I'm just going to hang here for a few days while you do whatever you're doing," Carmen said.

"I thought you came to help," Jamis said.

"When you blew up stuff, I changed my mind," Carmen said.

"I mean, she didn't blow it up. Some guy with an ax did," Sapphire said.

"Let's walk," Carmen said.

"Yeah, who was he?" Jamis stopped in the middle of the street. Her shadow stretched across the cobblestone. A car honked and Jamis held up her birdie finger and stood where she was.

"Oh my God, Jamis, just move," Sapphire said and grabbed her arm. "People have guns in Arizona."

"But who was he? I feel like I just forgot about him, or I keep forgetting about him," Jamis said.

"You know, you're right, actually," Sapphire said and let go of her arm. They stood under a canopy sign for a candy store. Levi wandered inside. Carmen followed him.

"Like, I'm having a hard time remembering exactly what happened, like it's there, but like a dream, just outside my conscious mind. Like when I forget a name or song title and struggle to find it," Jamis said.

She felt deep and unsettling anxiety. Inside, she reached for something, a thought, word, or understanding, but it was like falling from a great height. The harder she tried to find what she was looking for, the more elusive it became. Which was oddly a lot like life.

"You're in deep thought over there," Sapphire said. Jamis heard her but wasn't ready to leave her own thoughts yet. Was there a real live killer involved too? Was that why the Phoenix police were involved? A shout startled her, followed by the squeal of tires. Down the street, a man yelled at a young child who rushed into the street. A car stopped just in time. In the chaos after the event, numerous other people rushed to the man and the child, gathered around, hands covering their mouths, aghast, chattering.

Sapphire and Jamis stood shoulder to shoulder watching the scene unfold. The person driving the car climbed out and waved his arms wildly. "Sorry," was heard again and again, but the background noise of everyone's conversations drowned out the rest of what was said.

Jamis stepped toward the fray, pulled forward by the same restless anxiety that propelled her introspection earlier. She was looking for something but didn't know what. She was too aware of the beating of her heart and when she tried to swallow, was not able.

That's when she saw him across the street, when the swallow was stuck halfway down her throat. He wore the same baseball cap he wore in the desert. They stared at each other. He acted as if he was expecting her. Jamis charged toward him and he retreated into the crowd. She pushed, turning in circles to try to find him. At the edge of the overlook point, Jamis scanned the descent and then looked up and down the street.

Sapphire waited for her across the street, hands in the air, waving for her attention. Jamis rushed to her.

"Guy from the desert," Jamis said, struggling to remember him again.

"Levi is gone," Sapphire said. She pointed up the road at Carmen's retreating figure. "She went that way to try to find him."

"What do you mean he's gone?"

"I mean, Carmen turned around in the candy store and he was gone. Vanished. Departed," Sapphire said, emphasizing the final two words. Then, she said, "I told you."

"He could be in danger," Jamis said. Sapphire tipped her head and pulled a face, lip curled. "You go down that way. I'm heading up the hill."

Sapphire nodded and took off down the one-way street that careened into some empty and abandoned buildings. Jamis climbed a set of stone stairs to the crowded street above. Like the street below, it was one-way, filtering traffic through the tiny town. She slowed, evened her breathing. Her ribs ached and she held them, struggling to find her center.

She closed her eyes and reached outward with her mind. It was like venturing for a walk in the sun, each step carrying her farther from safety but closer to something new. Jamis read about astral projection in a book by Madam Blavatsky. She'd practiced it during her recuperation. She was cautious though because prior to this, her only experience with consciousness projection was from Johnna's couch to the barn, and it never worked. Necessity required her to try it now, and from her right, a sensation tickled her awareness and she turned toward it. Levi stood in front of a stone building, next to a sign that read, "Ghost Hunting Tours." Maybe she could work it, when needed. Or maybe her peripheral vision registered Levi in her unconscious mind before she became fully aware of him. How she could be so skeptical and still chasing ghosts she didn't know.

Jamis walked to him, her pace quick. Levi didn't acknowledge her. He stared ahead, eyes glazed and unfocused. He looked like he did in the car the night before. Jamis stood about six feet away from him.

"Levi," Jamis said. He didn't respond. She repeated his name again. He glanced at her and she closed the distance between them. "Snap out of it, Levi."

Recognition dawned in his eyes. "Jamis, help me." Jamis took his large arm in her hand. The pressure she applied worked. He looked over her shoulder and then behind where he stood. "Where am I?"

"Jerome," Jamis said, unsure of how confused he was.

"I know that, but how did I get up here?" He pointed at the sign behind them.

"We lost you. You just disappeared. We split up to find you," Jamis said.

"Ghost hunting. Isn't that what you do?" Levi kept pointing at the sign.

"It does seem quite ominous, right?" From behind, she heard voices shouting her name. It was Sapphire and Carmen. Jamis turned to wave.

"Found him," she yelled.

"Obvi," Sapphire said. They joined them on the sidewalk.

"I think this is our next step," Jamis said.

"It's yours. I want a hotel room," Carmen said.

"We should all get one. So we're not stranded," Sapphire said.

"I don't have any money. I was going to sleep in my truck," Levi said.

"I'll get it," Jamis said.

"You don't have to. I'll be fine. I lived in my truck for six months once," Levi said.

"That's so sad," Sapphire said, her energy warming to him.

"Bleeding heart," Jamis said and nudged her with an elbow jab. Sapphire ignored her. Levi wiped a tear from his eye.

"I'm so confused," he said. Jamis was overcome again by a sense of responsibility for him. His aloneness felt a lot like her own.

"We'll figure it out," Jamis told him. He burst into tears. Jamis patted his back. "There, there," she said. Then, she giggled, an uncomfortable reaction. Sapphire glared at her. Levi looked betrayed, tears streaming down his face.

"I'm sorry. I giggle when emotion feels uncomfortable. It's a horrible habit," Jamis said, laughing. She bent over, hand on her ribs. "God, my sides ache." But then she laughed even harder and Sapphire started laughing too. It wasn't normal laughter, more like a pressure cooker venting steam. Carmen laughed as well, and finally Levi joined them. The four of them stood on the sidewalk, laughing until a sharp clack of thunder startled them into the dense reality of their present circumstances. Clouds moved rapidly in from the south, the sky darkening. There was the slightest hint of rain in the smell of the air.

Jamis wiped her eyes. "Hotel," she said. They followed Carmen to a corner hotel across the street. It felt familiar to Jamis, and when they stepped inside, she recognized it from her visit with Maggie. Carmen hit the bell on the counter. Sapphire studied black-and-white photos on the wall. Levi wiped his nose with a tissue from a box on a small table next to a couch.

A woman came through a swinging door. Her long black-and-gray hair was pulled up in a loose bun on her head. "Hi there. Need a room?"

Carmen stared at her, silent. Jamis shifted to her side and waited for her to speak. She didn't, but she did stare uncomfortably at the woman behind the counter.

"Carmen," the woman said. She stared at Carmen, frozen and transfixed.

"Lucy," Carmen said, a blush stealing up her cheeks. Jamis leaned closer to her to confirm.

"Okay," Jamis said with a whistle. "Don't mean to intrude, but we need four rooms." Carmen yanked her gaze away from Lucy and looked at Jamis. "Don't worry, I'll talk." Carmen nodded as Lucy turned away.

"It's busy. I can only give you three rooms. But they're doubles," she said apologetically.

"I understand. We'll take whatever we can get," Jamis said. Still Carmen stared, silent.

"I'm hungry," Sapphire said from behind them, oblivious to whatever was going on between Carmen and Lucy.

Jamis turned and mouthed to Sapphire, "I think they were a thing."

"What? Who was a thing? I'm hungry. I can't think," Sapphire said.

Lucy finished and gave Jamis three keys. She kept her eyes down and Carmen retreated to the end of the counter, hands shoved in her pants pockets.

"Thanks," Jamis said and handed Sapphire, Carmen, and Levi a key. "We can share?"

"Yeah, that's fine. Let's freshen up before we go eat or do anything else," Sapphire said, her big purse hoisted on her shoulder. Inside, Jamis knew there was a laptop, iPad, two phones, a variety of cables and other devices. She also traveled with a full medical kit and medical marijuana wrapped up in tiny candy that looked like toffee.

Levi dutifully followed Jamis down the hall. They stopped, waiting for Carmen, but she'd returned to the center of the counter and was talking to Lucy.

"You coming, Carmen?" Sapphire waved at her.

"Go ahead. I'm going to catch up with Lucy a bit," she said.

"Yeah, she's catching up," Jamis said.

"Huh?" Sapphire stopped on the stairs to look back over her shoulder.

"They know each other and I think it's in the Biblical sense," Jamis said, telling her Carmen's reaction at the counter.

"No way," Sapphire gasped, gleeful.

"I'm real happy for her," Levi said, weighing in, obviously feeling left out. "Lucy is pretty."

"She is," Jamis said as they opened the doors into the hotel room. "Let's meet back downstairs in thirty minutes."

Inside the room, Sapphire said to her, "Do you feel like we're being a bit too chill about all this?"

"Yes. I keep forgetting why I'm here," Jamis said.

A sharp bang from the bathroom interrupted their conversation and Jamis moved toward it. Sapphire stayed where she was, stretched out on the bed. Jamis opened the door, turned on the light, and found only emptiness. Inside, she studied the space. There was a small bathtub with an antique shower head and a wire rail on the ceiling for the shower curtain. The toilet was normal, but the sink was an antique pedestal. Jamis saw herself in the small mirror on the wall. There were dark circles under her eyes and her hair looked greasy. She should shower and delay meeting back up until after she took more care cleaning up. But her bags were in the car, parked down the hill.

She rubbed her eyes with her hands, and then rinsed her face with cold water from the tap. She used a washcloth with a bit of complimentary soap to wipe her arms and neck. She stuck her face under the faucet. As she came back up to her full height, to stand in front of the mirror again, she froze. There was a figure dressed in a scarlet red suit behind her. His face shifted in and out of phase, but she knew it to be a man based on his height and build. Jamis knew if she turned around he would be gone, so she held still.

He touched her shoulder with his hand and Jamis grimaced. It felt like a soggy rag. He whispered in her ear. "They're just waiting for you to die and join them." Then he was gone and Jamis was alone again.

Fear was parked in her chest like an idling two-ton pickup truck. Jamis dried her face and left the bathroom.

"Um, Sapphire," she said. But Sapphire didn't hear her. She slept on the bed, snoring.

They stopped to eat at the hotel restaurant, sans Carmen, who texted and said she was eating lunch with Lucy. Levi ate a hamburger voraciously and both Sapphire and Jamis ate veggie burgers with fries.

"But why a red suit?" Sapphire said in between bites. "That's weird. Who wears a red suit?"

"Right? It was weird," Jamis said. Between chasing down Levi, finding a hotel room, and ghosts in red suits, she felt like she was just running in place. "We've got to get focused."

"Yeah," Sapphire agreed but said nothing else.

"Let's go where Levi was led, see what's up there. And that guy," Jamis said.

"Oh my God. The guy with the ax," Sapphire said, hand on her mouth.

"We keep forgetting him. Maybe there is some sort of spell on him. Like you see him when he's there, but then when he's gone, he drifts from your conscious mind," Jamis said.

"Is that possible?" It was Levi, eating his second hamburger.

"Maybe? I think it's like a cloaking spell," Jamis said.

"I'll see what I can find about things like that," Sapphire said.

"Meanwhile, we should keep reminding ourselves of him. He could be dangerous," Jamis said. They finished eating in silence.

As they left the restaurant, a steep staircase caught Jamis's attention. A server saw her and walked to stand next to her. "Creepy, right?"

"Yes," Jamis said, surprised. She didn't look at her though because her gaze was fixed at a point at the top of the stairs where the woman from her dreams stood, dressed in a black Victorian dress with a veil. She uncovered her face and smiled at Jamis. It felt too familiar and Jamis shuddered, frozen. Then, she blew a kiss to Jamis and the noise of restaurant faded away.

Jamis was no longer in the twenty-first century. The door behind her opened and dust blew in from outside. A horse galloped by and then a carriage behind it. The woman was no longer at the top of the stairs but next to her. Jamis took a quick few steps back and stumbled. The edge of the wall struck her between her shoulder blades, and she cried out.

A man in tan pants and boots turned in her direction. "Did you hear something?" He spoke English, but the accentuation of words sounded different to Jamis's ears.

"Nothing," the woman said, glaring at the man. "Now tell me what you came to tell me."

"Gareth Hamilton is riding this way at sunrise tomorrow. He brings a posse of men with him. I heard he plans to see you hung," the man said. He held his hat against his chest, in deference. A ring of dirt crusted sweat showed where the hat rested on his head. His hands were filthy. There was dirt caked under his nails.

"We'll see if he can," the woman said and walked through Jamis to climb the stairs. The sensation of it ricocheted through her, like a pinball in a machine, bouncing back and forth, cold and heavy. The man dutifully followed the woman up the stairs. Jamis followed them, holding the banister to steady her ascent. There were voices in the rooms downstairs. Laughter. Upstairs, grunts and shouts, squeaking bed rails.

It was sex and she was in a brothel. The energy of the space was heavy, hard, and suffocating. Depravity and despair hung in the air, like it was sprayed from a bottle. Jamis paused and looked around. The people around her were shadows, not quite in focus.

The woman stopped in front of a door. "Did I invite you up, John?"

"No, ma'am, I just was following, well, I didn't mean to," the man stammered, clearly terrified.

"Go then," she said, and the man rushed away, down the stairs. Jamis watched him go. "But I don't want you to go," she said to Jamis, looking right at her for the first time. "You can stay."

Jamis's steps were tentative as she moved forward, hand on the wall, still uncertain of her whereabouts. Was this a vision and she was really walking up stairs and down hallways in the present day, while Sapphire hung on to her arm and begged her to stop? Or had she truly slipped through time?

"It's neither," the woman said.

"What? How did you—" Jamis wasn't able to finish her thought.

"I hear you thinking here," she said.

"I'm really here?"

"It's the only place any of us really ever are," the woman said with a smile. "It's what I figured out and why I'm still everywhere else I want to be."

Was this where Jamis had encountered Emma earlier in the year? In a dimension of eternal presence? Was she in the place where all is created?

"Lord, is it necessary to think about things this much? Isn't it enough that I tell you?" The woman leaned against the door, hands folded in front of her.

"I tend not to just take other people's word for it," Jamis said.

"Well, I can appreciate that," she said. She pointed to the room beyond the open door. "Want to sit and talk a bit?"

Jamis moved closer to her and peered over her shoulder. The room was dark, lit only by candles. The walls were covered in dark red-and-black fabric. There was a bed draped with silk black sheets. The woman pointed to a table painted black with red trim.

"I'll send for coffee," she said and took Jamis's hand and pulled her forward, but an equal force grabbed her other hand. Jamis was jerked from the room and the woman, who cried out in dismay.

Chapter Nine

Jamis opened her eyes. She was prone on the landing of the steps. Levi held her hand and Sapphire shook her shoulders.

"Wake up," Levi said, a whisper.

"This happens," Sapphire told him, and shook Jamis again.

"I'm awake. Stop it," Jamis said, struggling to sit up.

"Time stream slippage? Or dimensional portal?" Sapphire sat on the ground next to her and stretched, hands to her toes.

"Why are you so calm?" It was Levi, brow furrowed, concern in his eyes. "I mean, I'm possessed or something. She keeps freaking out. I want to go home but I don't have one."

"Yeah." Jamis pushed up from the ground and reached a hand down for Sapphire. "I saw that lady again."

"We need to find out who she is," Sapphire said.

"Let's keep going where we were going." Jamis moved down the stairs and met a surprised group of employees.

"We just called for help," one of them said.

"I'm fine. Just a ghost talking to me," Jamis said.

"Well, that happens here," he said, looking at the others who shrugged with disinterest as they moved away.

Jamis told Sapphire and Levi the details of her vision in route to the ghost hunting tour shop. Levi held the door for them, a heavy wood hung on iron that scraped the ground as it closed.

Inside, the lights were low. There was a glass shelf of mass-produced skulls directly in front of them. Postcards, shot glasses, and other Jerome tourist paraphernalia sat on shelves.

Jamis rubbed her eyes. They burned like they were doused in sand.

A young man about Levi's age approached them. "You need help?" He wore a T-shirt with the shop logo on it. Jamis turned toward his voice and he flung his hands in the air. "Oh my God, you're Jamis Bachman." He jumped up and down and called to a young girl behind the counter. "It's Jamis Bachman," he said, waving for her to join.

What followed was a flurry of activity, hugs, handshakes, a few autographs and selfies for other lingering shoppers before the energy settled back down enough for Jamis to ask questions. The young man's name was Devon and his friend was Blaire.

"I've been pulled here, for some reason," Jamis told them. She described the scene in the desert, Levi's abduction, and the events of the day.

"You left out the guy with the ax," Sapphire said.

Jamis turned to her. "Fuck me, I did." Her phone rang, and it was Johnna so she excused herself and stepped outside.

"So the explosion was actually caused by this guy with an ax…" Sapphire's words trailed off as the door closed.

"Hi," Jamis said, relief spilling through her.

"Blow anything else up?" Jamis smiled at Johnna's question and leaned against the plaster wall, put one foot up to balance her, and for an odd moment, wished for a cigarette. She'd not smoked for a long time, so it had to be the nonstop stimulation of the last twenty-four hours. She told Johnna of her vision and current situation.

"Oh, and Carmen is eating lunch with a woman it looks like she knew well before," Jamis added, hoping it would be okay.

"Like, know how?" Johnna's tone was light, curious.

"They seemed familiar," Jamis said.

"Wow," Johnna said.

"Yeah," Jamis followed up.

"Just wow. And some creepy lady is hijacking you in time? Should I feel threatened?"

"She's terrifying, honestly. I feel a little out of my league here. I mean, everything feels so ambiguous," Jamis said.

"You can't just come home, can you?" Jamis heard the sad resolve in Johnna's voice and decided to switch the subject.

"We've barely talked about you. How was your day?"

"Good deflection. Busy. I'm taking tomorrow off to help Sam with a surprise house project for Sapphire. And I got a text that your pod is coming."

"What's the project?"

"If I tell you, I know you'll tell Sapphire. It's a no go," Johnna said.

"I miss you," Jamis said. The words pulled the ache out of her and longing swelled inside her chest. The sensation was foreign, and while she felt like love was her karmic reward for surviving, at times like this the reality of how much she felt for Johnna overwhelmed her. What would she do when it ended?

"Johnna, don't dump me," she blurted, overcome with the fear of losing her. Darkness overtook her peripheral vision and what she could see narrowed down to a pinpoint of light. She was having a panic attack, standing on a road in Jerome, Arizona, chasing a poltergeist and a guy with an ax. Her chest tightened and she stumbled to a low block wall a few steps away. She sat and put her head between her legs.

"Jamis. Where did that come from? Of course I won't," Johnna said, her voice steady and serious.

"Everything ends," Jamis said, gathering her thoughts from the chaos drowning her.

"It does, Jamis, but for us, it's to the nursing home," Johnna said. She paused, quiet, and Jamis gathered her thoughts, breathing through the panic. Somewhere in the past twenty-four hours she'd lost her ground. "And who knows what comes after that," Johnna said.

"Right. Promise?" It was the hotel and Maggie in her dreams. Broken people could be mended, but they were always something different after. Somehow, becoming healthier had exposed a fragile, tender underbelly ripe with fissions, insecurity, and a need for constant validation.

"Promise. I love you. I've waited my whole life for you. I didn't even know I was missing a puzzle piece until I met you. Really, I just want to know where you were and what took so long," Johnna said.

"I'm sorry—" But Johnna cut her off.

"No. No sorry. Just figure this out and come home. I miss you, too. You okay?"

"Yeah," Jamis said, vision returning to normal. Her heart raced like a car stuck in park with a foot on the pedal, but she could stand again. "Let me go see what I can find out and I'll call you before bed."

They said their good-byes. Jamis tucked her phone away in her back pocket. There was a family across from her. Mom and Dad plus two kids. She watched them with forlorn longing and wondered if she'd ever be able to have anything so normal and stable. Dad picked up the daughter, spun her around, and Jamis smiled as she giggled. He sat her on his shoulders. They disappeared into the shade and around the corner of the building. In their place, was the man from the desert, ball cap pulled low. Jamis startled and stepped back in shock, falling back over the wall into a dirt garden bed of flowers.

Someone cried out. "You okay?" She felt hands on her arms. The dirt under her was soft and an orange flower covered her right eye.

"Yeah," she said, accepting help to regain her footing. As soon as she was on her feet, Jamis searched for the man. He was gone again.

An older man and woman stared at her. "You fell right back into that flower bed," the woman said.

Nothing like stating the obvious, but Jamis didn't say that. Instead, she smiled and shook their hands. "Thanks for your help." They nodded and continued on and Jamis went back inside.

She approached the group, mouth opened to talk, when Sapphire said, "What's in your hair?" She pulled the stem of a flower from Jamis's hair and handed it to her.

"I don't want to talk about it," Jamis said. Sapphire shook her head in a movement that conveyed resigned acceptance.

"We've been talking about what's happening, and Devon and Blaire are going to take us where Levi thinks we need to go," Sapphire said.

"Great. Where is that?" Jamis thought to brush dirt from her behind, and tried to do it casually, but Sapphire saw.

"Hold still," she whispered and helped her. It was all over her back, too.

"Well, really, it could be a couple of different places, so we thought we'd try with the old school first," Blaire said. She stared at Jamis with wide, curious green eyes. It was unsettling and Jamis turned away from her, still overstimulated from the events outside.

"Well, let's get going. Let's try to outrun the dark," Jamis said.

"Well, the dark makes it better," Blaire said.

"More activity?" Jamis took her vibrating phone from her pocket. It was a text from Johnna. *Don't panic. Find your ghost. I'll be here. I love you.* For so many songs, poems, and books written about love, very few of them got it right. Usually, they ended with consummation, a crescendo of relieved tension. But love was the commitment, surrender, and acceptance that came after. Jamis smiled, and a rush of emotion reminded her she was in earth school and mastery wasn't required. Just receptivity. Like everyone else, she was in progress and that was okay.

"Jamis?" She jerked away from her thoughts. Sapphire had said her name.

"Sorry, yeah, what?" She hadn't actually heard a word of what was said. A door closed loudly behind her and she jumped to look. It was just another customer.

"We're heading up to the closed down school first. That okay?" Blaire asked her, hand reaching across the counter for a ring of keys.

"Yeah, that's fine. Let's go," Jamis said.

The road wound down. If Jamis had reached her hand out the window, she would have touched the side of the mountain. The rock was flat where it was blasted to clear the way. They were in a black Hummer with bright green trim. Jamis learned in route that Devon and Blaire owned the shop and ran the tours. For them, Jamis was a revered expert, and their behavior with her was so deferential it made her uncomfortable.

Somehow, the day disappeared and the sun was setting. Twilight stirred to life and the bleak desert landscape was bathed in purple hues. Jamis closed her eyes and tried to remember how the day began. She'd been in the hotel room, in Phoenix, then the Uber to deal with the rental car and then Levi, then Jerome. She was exhausted. Sapphire was next to her, Levi on the other side.

They'd not heard from Carmen so Jamis texted her. *You all right?* A few moments later, Carmen sent her a thumbs-up emoticon, proving she did know how they worked, something Jamis would take up with her later. The car bounced as they turned off the paved road, descending onto a dirt road that wound back up the face of another mountain, toward an abandoned school.

"At one point, Jerome had over fifteen thousand people. It was a bustling mining community for copper. The Depression slowed demand, a lot, but then World War II came along and upped the demand again. After the war though, demand dropped, and since Jerome only existed for the mine, when it shut down, the population plummeted," Blair said.

"If I remember correctly, it became a ghost town as a way to survive," Jamis said.

"I guess in some ways it's the only marketable thing left, you know?" It was Devon who responded, as he shifted the car into park. The darkness outside was complete and Sapphire shivered. Jamis leaned against her to offer reassurance. "But while it's about survival, the thing is, it's real. Life here before the mines shut down was brutal."

Blaire nodded in agreement. "The mining companies saw miners like they saw equipment. If one was injured, they sent him up to the hospital. If the hospital could heal him so he could return to work, they did. If not, they medicated them, kept them comfortable with opium, let them die, and the company paid a flat fee to families for their life."

"That's why unions are still necessary," Sapphire said.

"Unions seem to be a pain in the ass," Levi said.

"You say that, but before the unions came in the early twentieth century, life was brutal, short, and hard. They're the only reason we have forty-hour work weeks, safety protections, vacation, or healthcare," Sapphire asserted.

"It's true. They worked every day, for twelve to fourteen hours, in unimaginable conditions," Blaire said.

"Without any notion of modern healthcare. Or antibiotics, vaccines, ibuprofen," Sapphire said.

"The Spanish flu decimated Jerome. There were so many victims, they ran out of places to bury the bodies and just started burning them. Some victims were tossed into the slurry. Some were ground up in the mix used for the building foundations."

"Fuck me," Jamis said.

"Yeah. There's a lot of unfinished business here, and a lot of restless spirits," Blaire said. She stared at Jamis. Once again,

Jamis found her gaze unsettling and odd, but there was nothing threatening about her. She was just weird and Jamis liked weird. "Sapphire said maybe your ghost is a madam?"

"I think so, yes," Jamis said.

"Well, their lives were as bad as the miners. Some women would see as many as eighty men a night," Blaire said.

"I'm going to be sick," Sapphire said.

"We're getting the gist. This was a hard place, with a lot of trauma, pain, and exploitation," Jamis said, intervening before she heard anything else. She opened the door and helped Sapphire down, but left Levi to fend for himself. He unrolled his long, gangly legs from the back of the Hummer and stumbled a bit.

"So this was a school?" Jamis strode ahead of Blair and Devon, curious and determined. She didn't see how it could possibly have anything to do with her scary Victorian lady but was still interested in seeing inside.

"The town raised funds for it at its peak, but eventually, it was shut down and it doubled as a hospital during the Spanish flu," Devon told her.

"This it, Levi?" Jamis stopped at the door that was boarded shut and peered in the broken windows.

"No, but the view is kinda like this," he said.

"Well, since we're here," Jamis said and with a small leap, moved from the front stairs to a windowsill before she stepped into the structure. There was just enough moonlight. "Got a flashlight?" she asked over shoulder and Devon rushed back to the vehicle.

"Um, Jamis?" It was Sapphire. She stood on the ground in front of the window Jamis was hanging out. "Whatcha doin'?"

"Just looking," Jamis said.

"Well, I was thinking maybe it's not a good idea to just rush into abandoned, derelict buildings but that's just me," Sapphire said.

"Scaredy-cat," Jamis said and leaned down to take the flashlight from Devon's outstretched hand. "Stay there, let me see if I can open the door." Moonlight cast an eerie light ahead of her. Jamis stood in place and pointed the flashlight all around. Broken boards lay across the stairs, partially obstructing the path. There was a gaping hole in the ceiling and an owl perched on a beam in the center of it. Jamis moved to the door slowly, watching for broken boards, and pushed. It scraped across wood and the owl took off in flight, startled by the noise, its wings beating against the night's unsettling silence.

Devon bounded in the door, followed by the more muted Blaire, Sapphire, and Levi.

"What are we looking for?" Jamis turned the flashlight to flood the foyer with light. Devon had another flashlight and joined her. A long hallway stretched before them, the end unknown. Their flashlights only shone so far. The hall dropped into darkness about thirty feet ahead of them, and Jamis shivered looking at it. Walking into it would be like walking into a black tunnel covered in fog, each step an act of courage.

Something rattled and they all jumped, forming a small circle without thinking, grouping together in the dark for safety. Doing so was an evolutionary defense mechanism. Jamis watched their behavior with fascination, wondering about human beings' capacity to bond so quickly in fear. Something fell, the sound coming from the direction of the darkened hallway. It was followed by another loud crash.

"I think we should leave," Levi said.

"Not yet," Jamis said, voice quiet. She left the safety of the group and walked to the top of the hallway. The flashlight didn't shine any farther into the darkness. She inhaled dust and dirt and coughed viciously. Sapphire came to her, forearm over her mouth.

"What are we doing here? It doesn't make sense. We only came to Jerome to have Levi take you where he saw in his dream,"

Sapphire said. Her desire to leave was evident in her voice, but her presence felt resolute at Jamis's side, as if to say, "I hate this, but I go where you go." Her friendship gave Jamis strength.

"I have no idea what I'm doing. None. I'm floundering around here, bouncing from one thing to another, just letting myself be led by strangers. It's not like me," Jamis said.

"I know. Let's regroup. Let's go back to the hotel, shower, eat, sleep, and do some research. I can query records about old Jerome. We can get more info from Levi," Sapphire said.

Jamis nodded, surrendered. She needed to listen. She felt like a boat unmoored from the dock, cast about in the water. Her head ached and she coughed again, turning to leave.

"Let's head out," Jamis said. But as she said that, the old school building shook and shrieked. A murder of crows landed on the beam where the owl sat. They squawked and fluttered their wings. A large feather floated in the air in front of Jamis. She lifted it from the air and held it between her fingers.

A swirl of dark red and black emerged in the darkness of the hallway, took the shape of a human, and then dissipated again. A translucent spirit dressed in a white hospital gown hovered in the air at the top of the stairs one moment, and the next, was in front of Levi, head tipped, eyes curious. He screamed and ran from the building, leaping through the window. Devon and Blaire held their ground. Sapphire grabbed Jamis's arm with both hands as they confronted whatever red-and-black shape moved in front of them.

"Is Levi okay?" Jamis called back to Devon and Blaire, not moving, eyes fixed on what was in front of her.

"Yeah, I think so," Devon said.

"Go check on him," Jamis ordered them. She didn't see them, but she heard their footsteps retreating.

"We should go," Sapphire said.

"Yeah," Jamis said, but neither one of them moved. Whatever was in front of them took a more cogent shape, the misty edges forming into an outline of a figure. Jamis took a small step forward. "What are you?"

But sirens behind her disturbed what was unfolding. Flashing lights flooded the space. She glanced over her shoulder, just briefly, to see cop cars outside. When she turned back, whatever was there disappeared.

"Cops," Sapphire said.

"Probably because we're trespassing?" It was a question more than a statement, but Sapphire didn't answer. Jamis stepped carefully outside to meet them and rubbed her arms against the chill. The temperature dropped with sundown.

"Jamis Bachman and Sapphire Nugent, I need you to come forward," a cop yelled. Jamis covered her eyes to block the glare of a spotlight turned on them.

"We're here, we're here. Maybe dial down the light," Jamis called to them. Mercifully, someone turned it off.

"What do you need us for?" Sapphire asked, hands on her hips.

"You're wanted for questioning in a murder," the cop said.

"Murder?" Jamis and Sapphire asked at the same time.

"Well, shit," Levi said.

CHAPTER TEN

Levi returned to the hotel to find Carmen and gather his emotions. The experience at the old school upset him. Devon and Blaire chatted with the police and apologized for being inside the school, but it seemed to be something they did often and after, slipped away as quickly as possible.

Jamis and Sapphire were taken back to a police station. It was in a small building on Main Street, not far from their hotel. The cops refused to tell them anything, but they didn't seize their phones so Jamis texted Johnna an update. Sapphire answered her phone when Sam called and talked to him while they waited.

After a thirty-minute wait, two well-dressed people came in and sat across from them.

"My name is Vera and this is Andrew. We're detectives with Phoenix police," the woman said. She wore her dark hair pulled back tight and a dark suit. She slipped out of the coat and put it on the back of the chair. Andrew did the same with his coat and loosened his tie.

"Why are we here? It looks like trespassing might be a bit out of your jurisdiction. And how did you find us at the school? I'm not sure what's going on," Jamis said.

"I don't know. The police chief here guessed, I think. Someone saw you with the locals. We're investigating a series of murders throughout the state. We found a body at the explosion site near Blythe, where you were," Andrew said.

"A body? Where? We had been there less than an hour when that happened," Jamis said, suddenly panicked.

Sapphire touched her arm. "Don't say anything at all. We'll see if we need a lawyer."

Jamis nodded and settled back against the chair, reassured by Sapphire's calm.

"Let's hope that won't be necessary," Vera said.

"Never know," Sapphire said. They stared at each other. "Go on." Sapphire waved her hand in the air.

"The body was found in the root cellar," Vera said.

"We didn't go in there. Charlie, the owner, and his sister, Gwen, told us the cops had asked them to not go in there," Jamis said.

"We spoke to them," Vera said.

"So they confirmed it. And you know they asked for my help," Jamis said.

"Yes, they did. They also had no idea there was a body in there," Vera said.

"Well, that's probably true," Jamis said. The room became quiet. The air stilled around them and something came to the front of Jamis's mind, a nagging thought just outside the grasp of her conscious mind. She sat back in the chair and put her arms up, laced her fingers behind her head, and stared at the ceiling. There was something important she should share but couldn't remember what it was.

"Are you okay?" It was Andrew. He leaned forward on his arms. The table squeaked with his weight.

Jamis didn't answer him, but Sapphire spoke. "There was a guy out there," she said, almost breathless, like she fought to get it out of her mouth.

Jamis brought her arms down into her lap and nodded, uncharacteristically quiet.

"A guy?" It was Vera who asked. Sapphire told her in a solid rush of words, not stopping, like she was afraid to forget again.

"And we keep forgetting him," Jamis said.

"Like how?" Vera asked, enthralled.

"Well, I think I saw him up here, across the street when we first got here, and then again, before we left for the old school. But I keep forgetting," Jamis said. They sat in silence, contemplating the strange man who escaped their memories. "Do you think he's who you're looking for?"

"I have no idea," Vera said.

"We're dealing with a serial killer who disposes of bodies by setting them on fire in the middle of the desert. The bodies are mutilated prior to disposal which made forensics hard to gather," Andrew said.

Vera glared at him, likely upset he'd revealed so much.

"Wait, so there is a real live serial killer? And he blew up a body at Charlie and Gwen's?" Jamis was astounded and terrified. Ghosts were one thing. Serial killers were way out of her league.

"Well, it seems to be that there is some connection to your experience last night and the case we're working on. We think the explosion was a mistake, but not the burning of the body," Vera said.

"Are we suspects?" Sapphire's tone let them know the question was deliberate and their answer determined what came next.

"Not at this time," Andrew said and looked at his partner, who shrugged, then whispered in his ear. Jamis's phone vibrated. It was Carmen. She silenced it, ignoring the call. "Would you be willing to work with a sketch artist?"

"I don't see his face, at all. I can tell you he's taller than me, by about four inches, making him really tall. He's thin though. He wears a hat pulled down low," Jamis said.

"And jeans and a white T-shirt," Sapphire said.

"But that's it," Jamis said. She pulled Vera's notebook forward and quickly sketched him for her.

"You can draw," Sapphire said.

"Many talents," Jamis murmured as she finished up and pushed the notebook back.

"I don't think I need to tell you to be careful," Andrew said.

"If he's here—" Vera said, but Jamis cut her off.

"Yeah, we know. But how does he connect to anything else that's happening?" Jamis shifted, uncomfortable on the hard plastic chairs. Sapphire put her head down on the table.

"Tell us everything," Vera said.

"Right now?" Jamis wanted to go back to the hotel room and sleep.

"No time like the present," Vera said and Jamis sighed. She started at the beginning, with the email from Charlie.

It was after midnight when Jamis and Sapphire trudged in the hotel, legs heavy with sleep. Carmen waited for them in the lobby and rushed to them as they came in.

"Where have you been? Are you okay? I called the cops, but they told me you were there," Carmen said.

"Yeah, apparently there's a real-life serial killer on the loose," Jamis said and told Carmen the story. A part of her knew she should be more worried, but her tiredness superseded her good sense.

"You need to sleep," Carmen said.

"And eat. I'm starving again," Jamis said.

"Me too, but I don't even know if there is anything open this time of night," Sapphire said.

"I'd take a vending machine," Jamis said.

"Hold on," Carmen said and stepped through the door to the office behind the counter. A few moments later, Lucy came out with her.

"I'll get you something warmed up in the kitchen if you want," Lucy said to them, and made shy eye contact from behind her glasses.

"It's so late. You sure you don't mind?" Jamis liked her. She reminded her of her fourth grade teacher, whose name escaped her.

"Not at all. I'm up," she said. They followed her into the restaurant and Jamis punched Carmen's arm as they walked, winking.

"Shut it," Carmen whispered with a smile.

They took the table closest to the kitchen. Sapphire tried to help her, but Lucy refused. She'd turned on just one set of lights above the bar, so the room glowed with amber light. Jamis closed her eyes and savored the scents and sensations of the moment. The hotel was quiet. The room empty, except for her friends. For the time being, she was safe from whatever mystery had pulled her in. When she opened her eyes again, even the dark wood of the bar was comforting.

Since she'd met Johnna, Jamis had learned to appreciate slowing down and disconnecting. Johnna never used her phone for anything other than talking and the occasional text message. She read real books. Listened to the radio. After Sam moved out, Johnna actually forgot to pay the Wi-Fi bill and couldn't remember where the router was.

She would have loved the hotel and Jerome, and Jamis missed her ferociously and paused to text and tell her so. The sounds of Lucy behind the swinging door crept into the silence. Johnna texted back a sleepy message and Jamis promised to call in the morning. Sapphire was behind the bar and switched on an old radio. Soft jazz filled the quiet space, broken only by the DJ's lovely voice before another song played.

Everyone was content to sit in silence and feel the comfort of the room and music. Carmen looked more at ease than Jamis had ever seen her. Sapphire's shoulders relaxed of all their tension and she stared at the table, lost in thought. Levi disturbed their peace for just a moment when he rushed to them, excited to see them. But even he was observant enough to pick up on the energy of the room. He sat next to Jamis and slumped in his chair.

Lucy came from the kitchen with a warmed up loaf of bread and a bowl of pasta, tossed with olive oil and veggies. She left it for them in the middle of the table, and for a moment, Jamis wondered who should go first when finally, Sapphire broke the stalemate.

"Suckers," she said and spooned the pasta onto her plate. They all followed her lead. Lucy returned with a bottle of red wine and a chocolate cheesecake. Levi opened the wine and poured it for them. They fell into grateful silence.

The clock turned over to one, and Jamis yawned, prompting the whole table to yawn.

"You know, it's just been one and a half days since our plane landed in Phoenix. Does that seem weird? Doesn't it seem like longer?" Jamis folded her arms in front of her and rested against the table.

"So much happened yesterday. And nothing at all," Sapphire said.

"We should get some rest and figure out what we're doing tomorrow morning," Jamis said. She thanked Lucy for the meal. Outside, in the hall, Jamis remembered a moment from her time at the hotel with Maggie. The déjà vu came upon her as she turned to step up the stairs. She took a few steps, trying to ignore the sensation but couldn't and so came back down to the hall. There was a picture at the end of the hallway. It might have been the same one that was there years before. The hallway was lit with soft, yellow light. She went to the picture, each step triggering a deeper sense of familiarity.

Her steps were light against the red-and-black carpet. It looked like the pattern she'd seen during her flashback in the restaurant earlier in the day. Or was that yesterday? Time was elusive and the fabric of reality felt elastic, revealing itself as it really was—collections of swirling atoms, moving slow enough or fast enough no one noticed. Jamis was sure she walked down the hallway, but it felt like she floated. Then, she was in front of a framed photo. It was the woman from her visions and dreams. Her brilliant blue eyes looked alive in the painting.

Jamis had seen it before, all those years ago. She remembered now. When she leaned against the wall, it had disappeared and that's where she'd seen the man in her dream the night before, when he was consumed by something following him. It all came together inside her mind, like a rubber band stretched to fit around a box, snapping. All the pieces fell into place, and Jamis knew her visit to Jerome wasn't arbitrary.

She touched the wall to test its solidity and to balance herself. As she did, a tall plant shifted just enough for her to see a name plate at the bottom of the portrait.

It read *Ned and Idana Doolan, 1883.* Jamis stared at it, transfixed. Idana stole into her dreams and somehow exerted control over the material world. A spirit materialized for Charlie and Jamis to warn them of her. Jamis had seen her, as though standing next to her. Her eyes were brilliant blue and her charisma undeniable.

But who was she? In the end, all humans were just portraits and pictures. Eventually, everyone became just a name on a census, in a registrar, or an image in a painting. That wasn't what was striking. What mattered was Idana had somehow managed to surpass the limitations of death and remain attached. She'd not come to Jamis to ask for help with unfinished business.

If she didn't want help, what did she want?

The light flickered around Jamis and something shimmered into existence next to her, but when she turned, it was gone.

"Jamis," Sapphire called behind her.

Jamis took her hand from the wall and took a few steps back. "I know who she is. The woman. And I've seen her before."

CHAPTER ELEVEN

The stairs had felt insurmountable. Jamis was stretched across the bed. Sapphire sat on the bed next to her. She took off her glasses. There were dark circles under her eyes Jamis felt responsible for.

"Why do you hang out with me?" Jamis rolled to her side, tucked a pillow between her knees, and watched Sapphire get comfortable on the bed.

"Hell if I know," she said, resting so she faced Jamis. Jamis smiled. "I just love you. Trust you. Think what you're doing is worthwhile, and not a lot of what anyone does these days is worthwhile." They fell silent for a few moments. "Idana Doolan is our scary lady then. That actually gives me something. When we wake, I'll go find what I can about her. But not until I sleep."

"Yes, please, sleep. I'm so exhausted," Jamis said, closing her eyes as she spoke. Sleep came fast, but it wasn't restful. Somewhere, in her consciousness, Jamis stayed aware. A real-life killer lurked, Idana could show up at any moment, and she'd brought her friends along for the journey, something that might prove to be a horrible mistake.

In her dream, she was outside Johnna's house. She could see Johnna's silhouette in the window of the guest room in the front of the upper story of the house. It looked like Johnna was changing the guest room sheets. Jamis smiled and tried to walk up the stairs into the house but was blocked. An invisible boundary separated her from the house. Jamis backed up into the yard, thinking she would run to challenge the barrier. Upstairs, behind Johnna's silhouette was another. It was large, and it stood behind Johnna while she worked, not moving until the arm raised above its head, a knife visible.

Jamis screamed and ran at the front steps again, only to bounce back into the gravel. She picked up rock after rock and threw it at the top window. The glass shattered and she heard a scream. Something jarred her from behind and then shook her, but she kept standing to run at the stairs, again and again.

Sapphire's voice found her and Jamis grabbed hold of it, tried to make it out while she beat against the barrier to Johnna's house.

"Jamis, wake up, you're dreaming. Jamis, wake up!"

She was dreaming again. Of course she was. How didn't she know? She had to open her eyes. She fought through her sleep, her body heavy, and opened her eyes. Sapphire was next to her on the bed, in a darkened room, in a hotel in Jerome. It took a moment for her sleep paralysis to wear off, but when it did she jumped from the bed to find her phone and call Johnna.

"It's the middle of the night," Sapphire said, confused.

"I need to know she's okay," Jamis said. The phone rang with no answer. She hung up and dialed Johnna's landline. It rang three times and Johnna answered before the fourth. Jamis breathed out all the terror she'd held inside.

"Jamis?"

"Are you okay? I had this dream," Jamis said.

"I'm fine. Just sleeping," Johnna said. Jamis closed her eyes and imagined the bedroom, tidy and under furnished, the long wall of windows open to the high desert beyond. She wanted to be there, with her. Virginia was probably curled up against her. Was Johnna in danger? Or was her subconscious just manifesting her deepest fears for processing?

"Did you lock the doors? Please turn on the lights and look around the house," Jamis said.

"Hold on," Johnna said and Jamis heard the rustle of the bedding and the sounds of Virginia's nails on the wood floors. "Everything is locked up. I'm all alone. What is going on?"

Jamis told her and she heard Johnna's sigh on the other end of the line. "Jamis, this is crazy. All of you need to come home, now, and let this go. I can get behind ghost chasing but not serial killers."

It was the first time Jamis had heard Johnna's voice so firm and it startled her and evoked a sense of rebellion. She'd do what she wanted, like always. But Jamis paused. If she was going to be involved with someone, it wasn't just about her anymore.

"I'm just glad you're safe. Let's talk about the rest tomorrow morning," Jamis said.

"Try to sleep," Johnna said.

Jamis hung up the phone and looked at Sapphire. "I think she's annoyed with me."

"Well, you're kind of annoying," Sapphire said.

"Thanks?" Jamis held up her hand in deflection.

"I mean, come on, Jamis. You're not stupid. This is a lot. And Johnna keeps stuff simple. It's a coping mechanism for her, make no mistake. Her life was simple, predictable, tidy and clean, and you come rolling in with all this energy and chaos. She's going to get overwhelmed by you. Maybe you should avoid calling at three in the morning. Now leave me alone so I can sleep," Sapphire said. She turned on her side away from Jamis.

Sapphire was right and Jamis knew it. She collapsed back on the bed. What if someone were there, and Johnna was in danger, and she hadn't warned her though? What then? It was the awful absurdity of the universe that tidy people fell in love with messy people, and introverts fell in love with extroverts. And that everyone was so damaged their bullshit crashed into each other once intimacy was breached. Jamis crossed her legs at the ankle and her phone buzzed. It was Johnna. *I'm sorry. I love you. Talk tomorrow. Please be careful.*

Shocked by her quick follow-up, Jamis felt the intense emotion building in her dissipate. *I'm a lot of work. No apology needed. I love you.* Johnna sent back a heart and Jamis plugged her phone back in, setting it on the nightstand, close enough to reach.

Because she couldn't help it, Jamis picked up the extra pillow on her bed and threw it at Sapphire. Sapphire didn't react except to put the pillow behind her back. But Jamis heard her chuckle.

Sapphire and Jamis sat at the small table in the hotel room. Both had showered and dressed. They were waiting for room service. Sapphire tapped into the hotel's wireless network when the guest access had proven too slow for her. She had a laptop open and connected to a tablet. There was a black screen open with lines of green data.

"Let's see what I can find about Idana," Sapphire said.

"Where are you looking?" Jamis folded a piece of paper smaller and smaller. She felt more rested and cautiously grateful that the night passed without any additional dreams. The relatively normal conversation with Johnna a few minutes before was affirming, even as she struggled to reassure her they were safe. The truth was they were not safe, and she didn't think leaving now would solve anything. Idana had proven she could get Jamis where she wanted her. After realizing she'd seen her picture all those years ago, Jamis felt even more committed.

Sapphire didn't answer her, but she was focused. Jamis dug around in her bag for her laptop and posted a status update on social media, conveying details of her visit to Arizona, sans the information about the explosion and serial killer. Instead, she wrote about the abandoned school and added photos she'd snapped absentmindedly of Jerome since they arrived. It was the first post she'd made in a few days and immediately, notifications lit up. She closed the browser.

Finally, Sapphire spoke. "Okay, so Idana Doolan was born in Philadelphia in 1852 as Idana Drake."

"Idana Drake. That makes her forty in the picture downstairs," Jamis said.

"Right. She died in 1901, making it almost to fifty," Sapphire said.

"Old for that time, I guess," Jamis said.

"Crap, she was hung," Sapphire said.

"What?" Jamis scooted to peer over her shoulder.

Sapphire pulled a newspaper article up on the screen. "Yeah, check this out. She was hung for unspecified crimes against humanity and murder. Or so says the *Jerome Daily News* which ran from 1898 to sometime into the twentieth century."

"What does crimes against humanity mean?" Jamis tapped the table, anxious and thinking.

"I have no idea, but I'll find out," Sapphire said.

"Make that bigger?" Jamis pointed at the newspaper article. Sapphire did and Jamis read. "'Idana Doolan was sentenced to death by hanging for the murder of Jacob Monihan and other high crimes against humanity. Mr. Monihan was born in Philadelphia in 1857 and obtained his education at Harvard University before moving West to supervise mining operations on behalf of his family, who owned a majority share in Jerome Mining Company. Idana Doolan was married to cattle rancher Ned Doolan who died in 1885, preceding her in death.'"

"Idana was hung. Or wait, is it hanged? Hung?" Sapphire paused, thinking about it.

"Regardless, that's a pretty awful way to go," Jamis said.

"But what happened? I wonder if the tourist bureau or if Blaire or Devon know the story," Sapphire said.

"Maybe. You can't see anything else?"

"Let's see. Idana Drake Doolan. You said it felt like she was a madam in the flashback? Maybe there's something in local university archives. ASU, NAU, UA are all close by. Some of the historical records might even be in California. A lot of Southwestern history migrates there. Public libraries in metro Phoenix might have stuff too," Sapphire said, tapping on the keyboard.

Jamis opened the drapes to let natural light into the small hotel room and turned off the lights. The sun was high in the sky. It was close to ten, but they'd needed the extra sleep. They'd not heard from Levi or Carmen, and she wasn't in a hurry to wake them.

A knock on the door startled them. Jamis opened it to get their room service and made room for the tray on the dresser. She poured two cups of coffee and handed Sapphire one. Then she set their breakfast plates on the table so they could eat while they continued to search.

"I see plenty about Jerome but nothing specific about her or what her other crime is," Sapphire said, frustration visible.

"What about this living guy the cops are chasing? Who is he? What do they have on him? Can we find that out?" Jamis shifted gears to give them time to consider and think about their options before continuing with Idana.

"I mean, I could peek in the police files," Sapphire said.

"Sure, I mean, if we're polite and clean up after ourselves, what could it hurt?" Jamis grinned and Sapphire cracked her knuckles.

"It's perfect to do it here, too. I saw that they had to make a ton of connections to get data up here anyway, so it would be next to impossible to track a breach. Though they probably won't even know I've done it," Sapphire said.

"Because we'll take our shoes off, step lightly, and wear gloves," Jamis said.

"Not a trace of us behind," Sapphire said.

"I think we both stopped developing somewhere around the age of fourteen," Jamis said.

Sapphire giggled, tapping ferociously on the keyboard, and said, "Give me about forty minutes or so."

"I'll go find Levi, check on Carmen, and see what I can find out around town," Jamis said and finished her breakfast quickly.

"'K, and we'll reconvene when I have more here," Sapphire said.

Jamis slipped on her shoes and grabbed her backpack to leave. Just as she was almost out the door, Sapphire called out.

"Be careful, please."

Jamis gave her a thumbs-up as the door closed behind her.

Jamis found Levi downstairs in the restaurant. He was slouched in his chair, hand on his chin. His eyes lit up when he saw her and he waved.

"Did you eat?" Jamis asked before doing anything else.

"Lucy fed me," he said.

"Good. Want to poke around with me today?" He followed her from the hotel, and they were both momentarily disoriented by the bright sunlight and oppressive heat.

"Dude," Jamis said.

"Yeah," Levi agreed.

"Let's get something to drink first," Jamis said. They stopped at a walk-in for coffee and bottles of water.

"Okay, I need to find Blaire and Devon, and if I can't find them, I need to find the historical group, whomever they may be, but given that Jerome isn't too big, I'd say we can figure it out," Jamis said.

"Got it," Levi said. They made their way to the Ghost Hunter shop where they'd met Devon and Blaire the night before, but they weren't there. They asked for directions to a travel bureau or historical society, but when they got there, it was a shed with windows full of brochures. Jamis redirected them to the police station.

The doors opened to blissful air conditioning. No one was immediately present, but Jamis heard voices and called out. "Hello?"

Vera appeared in the doorway, wearing the same clothing she'd worn the night before.

"Jamis," she said.

"Vera," Jamis said. They stared at each other, an uneasy stand-off.

Finally, Vera blinked. "Did you need something?"

"Information on Idana Drake Doolan, hung here in 1902," Jamis said.

"Huh?" Vera rubbed her eyes. A woman appeared behind her.

"What do you need?" She spoke and Vera grew silent, watching Jamis with interest.

"I'm looking for someone who is familiar with local lore, history, etc. Can you direct me to someone who knows?"

"Hold on, let's see," the woman said and left. A few moments later, she came back with a piece of paper with an address and name. "They said to go here."

Jamis took the paper. "Thanks. Who is this?"

"A local who loves history and knows a lot about it," she said to Jamis.

Vera still watched her, though her gaze was unfocused and confused. "Why are you still here?" Jamis asked.

"We found another body around three," Vera said, but then stopped. Likely, she realized her breach wasn't prudent.

"What? Here? You found a body here?" Jamis's heart hammered.

Beside her, Levi said, "Well, shit."

"I shouldn't have told you. It has nothing to do with you," Vera said.

"Except that it does and with Idana Drake," Jamis said.

"You expect me to believe my killer is somehow connected to a woman who has been dead for what, one hundred and ten-plus years?"

"Ma'am, with all respect, I'd listen to her. Since I met her, I've been possessed and saw some spirit thing at the school," Levi said, interjecting.

"It is. I'm telling you it is. I don't know how or why, but somehow it's all connected," Jamis said.

"Then you're in danger because whoever this is, he's brutal. You should pack up, take your friends, and go home, wherever that is," Vera said.

"I need you to share what you know," Jamis said.

"You're kidding, right?" Jamis didn't answer. "Go home. Before I find your body." Vera left them with a wave of her hand, dismissing their concerns.

"Cops never believe me at first," Jamis said.

"I wouldn't have believed you if I hadn't experienced what I did," Levi said, face earnest. Jamis tapped the address into her phone and they set off for their newest destination. It was just a half-mile due west.

"Let's see what this person has to tell us about Idana Drake," Jamis said.

❖

The house was perched on the face of a mountain, braced on stilts. It had been painted a bright blue recently and stood out from its neighbors. Tiny figurines of faeries and mermaids lined the small walkway to the front door. The inner door was open, but the screen door was latched. Jamis knocked on it and the metal frame rattled.

"Hold on," a deep voice called out. Jamis dropped her hand before knocking again. A few moments later, an older man unlatched the door. "Can I help you?"

"Someone down at the police station gave me your address. Told me to come see you," Jamis said.

"You're the ghost hunter then," he said and waved them in. "I heard they picked you up at the old school last night."

"Word gets around," Jamis said.

"It's a small town with just a few locals," he said. Jamis and Levi sat on a worn leather sofa. He sat in an armchair across from them.

Jamis introduced them, waited for him to do the same, but when he didn't, she said, "What's your name?"

"Dr. Baxter Clemson," he said.

"Doctor of what?"

"Transpersonal psychology." Jamis made a kind of humming noise and averted her eyes. "You think I'm a quack, right? You're the one who chases ghosts."

His immediate assertion caught Jamis off guard and she squared up to him, sensing a challenge. Levi mumbled and turned away from both of them.

"I've just spent a lot of time in Southern California," Jamis said. Baxter stared at her. "I mean, everyone promises resolution for all your issues if you meditate on your trauma, drink algae spirulina smoothies with vegan protein powder, and talk to a life coach."

"Personally, I don't like spirulina," he said.

"Me either. What works for me is Klonopin," Jamis said.

"I've never been to California. I got my PhD online," Baxter said.

"So, I guess we're okay then?" Jamis was confused by the conversation.

"It just seems odd that someone like you would be skeptical of a holistic approach to health," he said.

"The thing is, I'm not. I think it's just how it's packaged," Jamis said.

"Um." It was Levi. They both looked at him. "We came to ask about someone called Idana Drake."

"Right," Jamis said, agreeing. "Do you know her?"

"Personally, no," Baxter said. He fell quiet and then he pushed off the chair and left the room. After a few more moments, he called out. "Come with me."

Jamis and Levi scrambled after him, crashing into each other as they got off the couch. Jamis impatiently waved Levi forward. They followed Baxter into a room at the back of the house. The wall in front of them was windows, above bookcases, overflowing with books. Jamis appreciated the spectacular view of the landscape beyond them.

Behind them were bookcases and a long wooden table that ran the length of the room. There were piles of books and papers on it. Baxter wasn't tidy. Jamis shifted a stack of books on the table, looking at them. They were wedding and funeral guestbooks from the 1970s. Jamis opened one and flipped the pages.

Baxter was looking at the bookcase and not at them. "Got those at an estate sale down the hill. Been digging through them," he said and Jamis closed the book.

"Sorry about that," she said.

"No, you're fine. I'd look too," he said. He took a book from the shelf and turned to them, motioning for them to sit at the table. Baxter took the seat across from them.

"Idana Drake was known as Idana Doolan," Baxter said.

"Right. It's her maiden and married name. I have a feeling she'd prefer Idana Drake," Jamis said.

"A feeling?" Baxter asked the question as he flipped through the book pages.

"A hunch," Jamis said.

"And yet you scoff at transpersonal psychology," Baxter said.

"I'm complicated," Jamis said. Baxter smiled without looking at her. Jamis wasn't sure she liked him, though she couldn't understand why.

"Here she is. It's odd, because someone else came by to ask about her, quite a few years back. She was writing a dissertation on women of the old west. I can't remember her name though. She'd run across her diaries at an antique consignment shop in metro Phoenix. But what was her name?" He spoke to himself.

"Someone else was looking for her?" Jamis wanted to take the books from Baxter's hands and look herself, but she breathed into restraint.

"Idana didn't show up in Jerome until after her husband was dead. He was a cattle rancher. Had a big place out toward California," Baxter said, finger touching the page of the book. Levi gasped. Baxter looked up. "That strike a chord?"

"Where is 'near California'? Assuming there is an exact location," Jamis said.

"There's even a map," Baxter said. He turned the book to face her. The pages were yellowed with time. But the image was clear. It was a hand drawn and photocopied map of Charlie and Gwen's property.

"This is unreal," Levi said.

"We were just there." Jamis told Baxter the story.

"It seems as though you and Idana have some unfinished business," he said.

"Tell me more about her," Jamis said.

"Well, her husband bought some of the buildings up here and owned the brothel. When he died, from what I see here, she left the ranch and came up here," Baxter said.

"Was she from money? I mean, how did she end up out here?" She wasn't learning enough for anything to make sense yet.

"I don't think this says anything about that. People came out West in those days to escape and then disappear. What I can tell you is that a reputation of debauchery followed her. Was it because she owned a brothel? Or for some other reason? That I don't know." He got quiet and settled back into his chair, arms crossed across his middle, and left the book open in front of him.

Jamis pulled the book to her. Baxter didn't seem to mind. The title was *Unauthorized History of Jerome, Campe Verde, Cottonwood, and Prescott* by Betsy Foster. Self-published in 1983, which took a lot of effort and money at that time. The book wasn't exactly definitive. But it was something.

"Amateur historian," Baxter said, as Jamis studied the binding and copyright page of the book.

"Yeah, but sometimes that's all you've got," Jamis said. She quieted and read the short entry about Idana.

Levi nudged her. "What's it say?"

"Do you mind if I read it out loud?" Jamis lifted her eyes from the book to Baxter.

"Not at all," he said.

"'Idana Doolan (Maiden Name: Drake) arrived in Arizona sometime in the late 1800s. She was born in Philadelphia in 1852. Idana married a cattle rancher, Ned Doolan, which is how she ended up out West. But nothing about her life before is known. Idana was known for her cruelty and callousness throughout the region, and even men were afraid of her. She commanded a small posse of men who undertook her orders without question, and her husband's wealth insulated her from consequences. When he died, his brother took the ranch. She left the ranch and moved to Jerome. In 1901, she was hanged for the murder of local businessman and mine supervisor, Jacob Monihan. She was also charged with crimes against humanity, though the exact cause of those charges is unknown."

Jamis finished reading and stared at the pages. A sensation in her head promised a dull headache would follow. She rubbed her eyes and felt really tired. She wanted to take a nap, but Baxter and Levi were watching her so kept on.

"This is what my friend Sapphire found this morning. This must be out on the web somewhere," Jamis said.

"Anticlimactic then?" Baxter still had his arms crossed against his chest. Late morning sunbeams showed the dust in the air. Jamis felt dirtier from having been in Baxter's home.

"Not entirely. We know she wasn't nice. Do you know any way for us to find out the name of the woman who came to see you before? With her diaries? Do you know anything else?" Jamis took a picture of the book and pages before sliding it back to Baxter.

"That's all I have. If I think of the woman's name, I can let you know. Leave your number," Baxter said.

CHAPTER TWELVE

Outside, the wind blew so hard, Jamis struggled to stand upright. She and Levi sought shelter against a building on main street. It ripped past them, like it was angry.

Jamis put one hand up to her eyes to block the dust. Levi did the same thing.

"You'd think after living in the desert my whole life, I'd be used to this wind," he said.

"Never," Jamis said.

"We don't really know anything," Levi said.

"Not true. We know Idana Drake was killed for some reason. That she lived at the ranch where we met. She owned a brothel, and based on my flashback, she lived there. She was vicious and tough, which I kind of appreciate," Jamis said.

"That's concerning. You're kind of scary," Levi said.

"Well, not really. I just like strong women," Jamis said.

"You obviously never met my mom," Levi said. Just then, a car horn honked. Jamis followed the noise. It was Blaire and Devon.

"Jamis," Devon called out, rushing to her. He stopped in front of her, a little breathless. "I'm so sorry about last night."

"Don't worry about it," she said. Blaire arrived at his side. "It all turned out. But do you know anything about Idana Drake?"

"Yeah, I was raised down in Verde Valley, you know, the little city before you climb up here, to Jericho Hill and Jerome," Blaire said. Jamis and Levi nodded, standing side by side now. The wind had momentarily stopped. "I just remember my grandma saying stuff like, 'If you don't go to bed, Idana Drake will get you and eat you.'"

It wasn't anything really helpful, so Jamis walked away. Perhaps she should have said something, been more polite. But she was lost in thought already. Everyone followed her anyway. She caught their reflection in the window of a store, her striding purposely back to Sapphire, with the three younger people tailing behind her, as if eager for her validation.

Idana was a scary, sadistic lady who lived in a brothel. Jamis couldn't blame her, not really. Living as a woman before emancipation and property rights must have been unbearable. Living as a woman in the twenty-first century was often unbearable, and Jamis owned all her own stuff. Women were still the more oppressed half of the species, raped, abused, and murdered so much the facts of it became wallpaper. She thought of Stephanie Gardner and clenched her hands. She hoped Bobby Reynolds burned in hell. Her thoughts drifted to Dan Abbey, at home after being released on his own recognizance, his bail posted.

Maybe she did appreciate a terrifying female poltergeist who devoured men. Was that wrong? Maybe her ethics were careening down a slippery slope, but damn if injustice didn't piss her off. She tried to imagine Johnna's response to it all. It would be more measured and calm. She'd suggest the entire human condition was one of suffering, in varying degrees, at its foundation. The systems built to sustain humans either made it better or worse. She probably wouldn't feel this white-hot rage at women's oppression race through her. Jamis wanted to tear something apart with her bare hands.

Why didn't Idana own that ranch? Why did she go to Jerome? Why were those women, really barely girls, expected to service man after man? Jamis kicked a metal trashcan fastened loosely to a stop sign with a chain, and it toppled over, pulling the sign with it.

"Whoa," Levi said and grabbed her arms just as she lunged after it.

She was furious. Nothing in the world was fair. Everything from the Constitution to local ordinances was power applied against her body, telling her what she could and couldn't do. Why should she have to pay to live anywhere? The gecko on the block wall across from her didn't pay for his spot on planet earth. How absurd human society was, how petty, how childish. Humans were the only species required to pay for their place on a planet they didn't ask to be born on anyway.

Jamis struggled against Levi and he let her go. She stormed from the sidewalk to the lookout across from them. The wind picked up again and blew dust in her eyes. A small rabbit hopped on the ledge, not far from her. She thought momentarily about picking up a rock to throw at it, put it out of its mercy before hunger and starvation got to it. It was this thought that yanked Jamis from her spiral. A glimmer of her own consciousness emerged in opposition to the impulse for cruelty. It was like climbing out of a hole, toward a light.

She took a deep breath and closed her eyes, focusing on restoring her calm. There was a woman's laughter. It was Idana. When she opened her eyes, Jerome was dusty and dirty. There were no cement sidewalks or cars. A horse and rider galloped by Jamis. Across from her, standing where she'd kicked over the trash can was Idana, dressed in black. She smiled at Jamis and stepped across the road to her, skirt hitched up.

In the sunlight, Jamis saw her age on her skin. She was beautiful in her maturity, and despite her rational mind telling her to be afraid, Jamis felt drawn toward her.

"Idana Drake," Jamis said.

"You've been digging around, I take it," Idana said and took Jamis's arm when she stopped next to her. They walked together.

"They said you're mean. Is that what that room was for in the desert? Sexual sadism?" It occurred to Jamis such directness might backfire.

"Well, that's private," Idana said. She spoke English but it was different from Jamis's. Not enough that she couldn't understand, but enough that Jamis had to really pay attention.

"People in my time are really obsessed with sex," Jamis said.

"They were in my time too. That's just humans," Idana said. Jamis stopped walking and turned to face her, hand over her eyes. "That was my husband, not me. It was his thrill."

Jamis didn't know if she believed her. "Why do you want my attention?"

"That's presumptuous," Idana said.

"What other conclusion can I make? Come on," Jamis said, flustered and annoyed.

"Just settle," Idana said and rubbed her arm. Jamis did and now that the initial shock of the woman wore off, she felt strangely comfortable with her, almost safe. "That's better."

"It's got to be reciprocal though," Jamis said.

"What does?" Idana put both hands on her shoulders so she could stare into her eyes.

"This back and forth. I need to know what you want from me. I won't just be yanked around," Jamis said.

"As if I'd try," she said. Jamis raised an eyebrow.

"Were those your thoughts I picked up right then?"

"Yes and no. You picked up my emotions and filtered them through your own mind," Idana said.

"There is no way any of that is in my mind," Jamis said.

"Humans are so arrogant, including you. You don't think the capacity for darkness lives inside you? We all have shadow impulses. Even you, Jamis Bachman."

"But hurting that rabbit," Jamis said.

"How is the rabbit different from a cow someone eats? Life is suffering. Isn't that what your lovely girlfriend says?"

"How do you know her?" The hesitant trust Jamis offered Idana retreated and was replaced with full-blown alarm. Sirens wailed.

"Settle. I won't hurt her or you. I sense your thoughts," Idana said. Jamis said nothing back. "She's there often. I'm happy you've found someone you think so much about." They kept walking and came to the end of the dusty street and stood in the shade of a wooden building.

"I sensed your emotions and my mind assigned thoughts," Jamis said.

"I suppose you could say that," Idana said.

"What else could I say?"

"Anything you want. When you're smart enough, you can justify anything," Idana said.

"Well, that's concerning," Jamis said.

"Why does it scare you so much? You know who you are. Willful. Defiant. Iconoclastic. Individualistic."

"For someone dead over one hundred years, you're remarkably up to date in terminology. But maybe not pronunciation," Jamis said.

Idana laughed and patted her check. "Well, a girl can't be perfect. Better get back."

"Not yet. I want to know about this serial killer," Jamis said, but then Idana and old Jerome was gone, and Levi stood in front of her.

"You having a seizure or something?" He jammed his hand in his pants pockets.

"Idana," Jamis said. She needed to find Sapphire.

❖

Jamis found Sapphire where she left her, hunched over the computer in their hotel room. Levi sat on the corner of the bed, clearly uncomfortable. He'd just met them and had his entire life turned upside down as a result. Jamis felt for him.

Sapphire didn't seem as concerned but did stop typing to listen to Jamis's story and the conclusions they gathered about Idana. Once Jamis was finished, Sapphire said, "Well, I did find this dissertation. It's what I was just looking at. I didn't get a chance to look at the police stuff yet."

"You mean the woman who asked our metaphysical PhD about Idana a few years ago? With her journals?" Jamis felt excited. It was the most promising thing she'd heard all day.

"I am only guessing. When I couldn't find anything in any of the online archives, I went to an academic journal site and did a deep dive. I found an abstract of a dissertation that mentions Idana. But it's not scanned and uploaded, for some reason, so we'd have to go to ASU's main library," Sapphire said. She began to say something else, but Jamis interrupted her.

"Did you get the author's name?" Jamis's energy was restless and intent. Her encounter with Idana was so unsettling she wanted to figure this out and be done with it.

"You're so impatient. Yes, I did." Jamis raised her finger and opened her mouth, but Sapphire shushed her. "And I emailed her, and yes, she already emailed back. She teaches at Maricopa County Community College and she's happy to talk to us."

"You're amazing," Jamis said.

"Yeah, I know," Sapphire said and turned to Levi. "What are your plans? Why don't you go home now?"

"God, that's so rude," Jamis said.

"What? I've been nice to him, but we don't need him tagging along. Plus, I'm still not sure I trust you," Sapphire said to him.

"I really don't have anywhere to go, and I was supposed to take her somewhere," Levi said. "In my mind, I saw a place, but I still haven't seen it."

"It wasn't the school then," Jamis said.

"I don't think so," Levi said.

"Which is why it's best you just let go of it," Sapphire said.

"If he wants to come, he can," Jamis said.

"Thanks," he said. Sapphire sighed and returned to the computer screen.

"I just don't think there is anything else to do here," Sapphire said.

"Let's head back down to Phoenix. I'll go find Carmen, see what she wants to do," Jamis said.

She left Levi with Sapphire, and heard, as the door closed, "Don't try anything with me. I'm little but I know aikido."

"I'm a victim here," Levi said, but the rest faded from earshot.

❖

She found Carmen in the restaurant downstairs. She and Lucy faced each other, sipping coffee. Jamis watched them for a while, smiling. Carmen seemed more alive than she'd been before. Lucy saw her first and waved her over.

Jamis took the chair next to Carmen.

"We're going to head back down to Phoenix. Chase a lead," Jamis said. Carmen looked surprised and then momentarily despondent. "You don't have to go, if you don't want to. I mean, we can make arrangements to get you to the airport."

"I can get you there," Lucy said. Carmen looked at her. "If you want to stay a while, I mean."

Carmen nodded, a slight blush up her cheeks. "I've got to get home soon, for Rex."

"Your sister has him, right?" Rex was Carmen's dog she pretended not to like, though Jamis knew better. Carmen nodded. "He'll be okay. She loves him," Jamis said.

"I guess I could stay a few more days," Carmen said and Lucy beamed.

"Okay, well you just text me if you need me," Jamis said and Carmen nodded. "How can I get checked out with you?"

"Don't worry about it," Lucy said.

"No, I insist. I took three rooms. Please." Lucy followed her to the front desk to resolve the bills. Jamis tucked her wallet away. "How do you know each other?"

Lucy looked up from her work on the counter, surprised. "We knew each other years ago, in Phoenix. I was madly in love with her. When we were very young. But she didn't give me the time of day."

"And now?" Jamis turned away from Lucy and watched Carmen at the table.

"I guess we'll see. But she strikes me as lighter somehow," she said.

"She is," Jamis said. They both watched Carmen flip through the pages of the newspaper, oblivious to them. "Don't let her get away."

Lucy smiled. "I'll try not to. Thanks for bringing her here. Quite the coincidence."

"Nah, not that. Synchronicity. Kismet. And maybe with the help of someone else who loved her," Jamis said.

"Who?" Lucy tipped her head, bright eyes inquisitive.

"I think you should ask her that. I bet we'll see each other soon," Jamis said.

She turned the corner to go upstairs without lingering in the hall. Jamis wanted to get her things together and get back to Phoenix without another visit with Idana. She took the stairs two at a time and back to the room quickly. Sapphire told her Levi was packing up his room.

Her things sat on the bed in a pile. Sapphire cleaned up after her while she was gone. They readied to leave and met Levi in the hallway. Downstairs, Sapphire and Levi said good-bye to Carmen. Jamis waited outside, hand over her eyes to block the sun.

A car careened around the corner, driving too fast for the small road and roared its engine. Jamis turned just in time and leaped out of its way.

"What the hell?" she yelled as it raced up the street, swerving back and forth. The driver must have righted themselves because the car's trajectory straightened a few hundred feet ahead and they sped around the corner. Jamis's attention left the car and drifted across the street. It was the man from the desert, ball cap pulled low. She thought about charging after him, but for once, common sense prevailed. He was probably a serial killer, with some odd, unknown connection to Idana Drake. He waved at Jamis and her heart hammered in her ears. She had nothing to defend herself with and thought briefly about buying a gun at the firearm store they'd passed in Verde Valley.

But she didn't know how to shoot it and Sapphire would have a fit. It was a pointless thought. She wasn't fundamentally opposed to gun ownership but wasn't on the NRA's mailing list either. And as a public figure, it would somehow probably leak out that Jamis Bachman bought a gun, and then where would she be? Canceled by leftists who loved her. Her social media would become a minefield of hate and accusation. Jamis closed her eyes. Worrying about all of this, right now, was not the most productive use of her terror. Idana had her already active mind in hyperdrive. She should take out her phone and take a picture of him. Then, she should run as fast as she could to the police station to see if the cops from Phoenix were still there.

She pulled out her phone, opened her eyes, and took a picture of an empty sidewalk. He was gone. Her eyes were not closed more than a few moments. Jamis looked around quickly to be sure he wasn't sneaking up on her. A voice called her and she fixated on it in an attempt to reset her calm.

It was Vera and Andrew. "Where's Levi?" Andrew's tone was strident and direct.

"The guy, from the desert, he was right there," she said, pointing across the street.

"Levi," Andrew said.

"What? I'm telling you we have to go. The guy who blew up the stuff in the desert," Jamis repeated, hoping they'd listen. Vera's gaze followed where Jamis pointed.

"Right now? You just saw him? The one you sketched?" Vera stepped toward Jamis and took off her sunglasses.

"Yes, that is what I'm saying," Jamis said.

"We don't have time for this," Andrew said. A slight tremor of annoyance flickered on Vera's face. "Where is Levi?"

"Inside," Jamis said, pointing. He pushed past her. "Wait, why?" He ignored her, but she chased after.

Inside, Jamis's vision was darkened by exposure to the sun. She could only make out silhouettes and stepped carefully forward.

"Levi Martinez, you're under arrest for murder," Andrew said and grabbed Levi, yanking his arms backward. He secured the handcuffs and read off multiple charges. Jamis lost track.

"What, no, I didn't do anything," Levi said, struggling.

"Don't struggle," Jamis said. Levi listened and met her eyes. Her vision was clearing. "I'll get you a lawyer. Don't say anything."

"What are you doing?" Sapphire grabbed her arm.

"It's not him," Jamis said.

"You don't know that," Sapphire said.

"I do because I just saw him across the street and Levi was here," Jamis said.

"Your loyalty is admirable, but misguided. We found Levi's DNA on two of the earlier victims," Vera said.

"What? Which ones? How? Levi, I know you didn't do this," Jamis said, turning around to face Vera.

"You can't possibly know that," Sapphire said and pulled Jamis backward.

Jamis wrenched her arm away from Sapphire and lurched toward Levi. "Where are your truck keys?"

"My pocket," he said. Jamis lunged and grabbed his jeans, pulling the pocket open far enough to get his truck keys.

"No, you don't," Vera said and grabbed them. "That truck is going in for processing. You keep pushing it and I'll arrest you."

"Not a word, Levi, listen, not a word," Jamis said.

Andrew pushed him from the hotel lobby. "You're going crazy," Sapphire said.

"No, I'm not. It's not him," Jamis said.

"Think about it for just a second. Calm down. Stop being so emotional. He abducted you. Maybe at a certain point he decided it was more fun to play along, be your pal. When you saw the guy with the hat when we got here, it was during that time when he disappeared. He stalked you to the hotel so he could get you somewhere," Sapphire said.

Jamis took three steadying breaths. It was a solid, logical conclusion. If it were true, Jamis invited the wolf into the den as a friend and they were lucky none of them were dead. But it didn't feel true and Jamis didn't think Levi was the man she just saw across the street and told Sapphire so.

"What if he's working with someone? Did you think that maybe he has a partner?"

This question made Jamis pause, because that could explain her seeing someone when she knew where Levi was. But the idea was just too absurd and terrifying. Something about Levi made her implicitly trust and want to help him. If she couldn't trust her feelings about him, what feelings could she trust?

"You need to listen to her," Carmen said, her voice calm and steady. Jamis made eye contact with her.

"I'm still getting him an attorney," Jamis said.

"Fine. Do that. But listen to us," Sapphire said.

Jamis decided not to argue anymore with the two of them. The case Sapphire made was solid and his DNA and fingerprints at a murder scene was something she couldn't explain yet. She still needed to discover what was going on with Idana, and maybe while figuring that out, she could figure out what was going on with Levi.

"Fine. Let's head back to Phoenix," Jamis said.

"I know you're just humoring me. But don't shut me out. Let's figure this out together," Sapphire said.

"You want me to come?" Carmen had her hand on Jamis's arm.

"No. Enjoy your time here. We'll text if we need you," Jamis said. She picked up the bags and left the hotel, her anger propelling her forward. Levi wasn't a murderer. He'd been set up and Idana had planned all of this. Levi was just a pawn in a bigger game and Jamis would win.

But first, she needed to know more about who she was playing against.

CHAPTER THIRTEEN

The drive to Phoenix was uneventful. Jamis ignored Johnna's phone call and her text. She couldn't take another person telling her she was crazy. Johnna called Sapphire who told her that Jamis was driving and she'd call her back. The tension between them grew into an invisible force field as they dropped into Maricopa County and Phoenix became visible.

"I need you to suspend your doubt and just entertain that Levi might be innocent," Jamis said.

"There is nothing happening, at all, that suggests I should do that," Sapphire said.

"You've had it out for him since the minute we met," Jamis said.

"He kidnapped you," Sapphire said and faced her.

"Well, right, but then he stopped when I talked him out of it," Jamis said.

"Because you're so powerful and almighty that you can talk down someone possessed by a demon." Sapphire's tone was strident and harsh.

"You didn't see his eyes," Jamis said.

"I did. When he manhandled you into the back of the squad car. This isn't healthy," Sapphire said.

"Fine. Then I'll drop you off at the airport and you can go home," Jamis said.

"I didn't say that. I hesitate to leave you on your own because your judgment is suspect," Sapphire said.

"I survived years before I met you," Jamis said.

"Seriously?" Jamis didn't answer Sapphire's sarcastic question. "You're being very unkind right now."

"You're not listening to me. I'm asking you to suspend your doubt for just a minute and pretend that maybe Levi isn't guilty. If so, why? What is his connection to Idana? And then, from that let us guide our line of thinking," Jamis said.

Sapphire turned away from her, put her chin in her hand, and stared at the window. When she didn't speak, Jamis said, "Fine. I'll take you to the airport. I appreciate the help you've given me."

"Fine," Sapphire said. And they drove the rest of the way in silence.

Jamis stopped the car outside the terminal at Sky Harbor International Airport. Sapphire left the car and took her bags from the back seat and disappeared without a word inside. Jamis watched her go with panic festering in every inch of her body. Sapphire had quietly texted her the name, number, and address of the woman with Idana's journals but hadn't said anything else.

She pulled back into traffic to leave the airport when Johnna called again. She ignored it and called her attorney. She assured her they'd send someone to Levi that day and keep in touch about the rental car she'd blown up.

Johnna called again, a few moments later. She answered it, reluctantly, closed down and defensive, ready to go nuclear. No one understood and no one would listen to her.

"Hi," Jamis said, holding the phone on her thigh, speaker on.

"Jamis please go get Sapphire right now," Johnna said.

"It's not a good idea. We're having a disagreement," Jamis said.

"Well, then talk it out," Johnna said. Jamis pulled into a parking garage and wound up to the top floor while she thought. "Are you there?"

"Yeah," Jamis said.

"She's worried about you. So is Carmen. They've both called me," Johnna said. Jamis put the car in park and turned up the air. She still hadn't spoken. Her words were caught inside behind the betrayal she felt at Sapphire's refusal to hear her out. "Please tell me what's going on."

Jamis did, from the beginning, and finished asserting Levi's innocence. "This is different from Stephanie. It's not a twenty-five-year-old murder. There's an active killer. This Idana doesn't seem to be asking for help. What does she want?" Johnna's even, calm voice soothed Jamis, and for a moment, she thought about chasing Sapphire inside the airport and going home with her. But she couldn't let Levi get framed for any of this.

"I keep asking myself that, and I don't know," Jamis said.

"Well, maybe we can just hit pause for a moment and try to understand." Jamis tried to imagine what Johnna was doing and wearing. "What worries me is you didn't take my call." Jamis heard the hesitation and concern in her voice. Was she being irrational?

"I don't want my intuition questioned," Jamis said.

"But I think it's possible Sapphire feels the same," Johnna said.

"Shouldn't you be on my side?" Jamis's face flushed and her heart felt vulnerable and exposed.

"Stop it. It's not about sides," Johnna said.

Jamis watched a large truck park. A man climbed out after wrestling a windshield visor in place. The sound of planes taking off and landing was deafening.

"Do you ever get angry?" Jamis asked her the question to buy time, to consider whether she could let go of her indignation at Sapphire and make amends.

"Sometimes. But I find it largely unproductive. Everything is just a problem to be solved. Isn't that what you say?" Johnna stopped talking and the world outside Jamis was silent. No planes, no cars, no noise at all. She looked from right to left and turned around to look behind her. "Do you want me to get angry? Ignore my call again and I will," Johnna said.

Jamis smiled and selected the FaceTime option, changing their audio connection to video. "Hi, gorgeous," Jamis said.

"You're so stubborn," Johnna said, smiling at Jamis. "But I'm relieved to see your face."

"I'm not that stubborn." They smiled at each other, the tension momentarily gone. "I'm sorry I ignored your call."

"You're allowed to do it about three percent of the time," Johnna said.

"Why three percent?"

"I mean, I could walk you through the complicated qualitative and quantitative statistical analysis I employed, but given how you feel about math, I think it's best you trust me," Johnna said.

"I should go get Sapphire," Jamis said.

"The two of you should stop fighting each other, acknowledge your differences, and use them to figure out what's going on," Johnna said.

Jamis knew she was right but wasn't able to admit it. She felt vulnerable enough. Letting down her defenses was harder than keeping them up. Adjusting her certainty to allow for other opinions was the most uncomfortable thing she'd ever done.

"I'll go get her," Jamis said.

"One more thing," Johnna said, finger up. "Can you tell me what you hear next? And when you get Sapphire?"

"I will," Jamis said.

"I've got to go, but let me know what's going on," Johnna said and blew her a kiss as she disconnected.

She felt childish, and it was probably because that's how she was acting. Willful. Defiant. Insistent upon her own certainty. Her group home counselors labeled her file with notes about her issues with authority and angry emotional outbursts when she didn't get her way. Adulthood and time had given her better coping skills, but she could be hard-headed in the best of circumstances.

She left the car and walked across the parking garage, the sun oppressive. Her breath was choked and shallow and she rushed to the stairs and into the sliding doors, welcomed by cold air. Sapphire sat on a bench, phone up to her ear. She was crying.

Jamis stopped just in front of her and waited for her to look up. When she finally did, she stuck out her tongue at Jamis and finished her conversation, not hurrying to hang up. Jamis didn't deserve it and she knew it.

Jamis joined her on the bench and looked at her phone while Sapphire talked. She'd barely checked social media during the trip and so replied to a few comments. Her heart wasn't really in it so her trolling felt insincere. She tucked her phone away. It was Sam on the other line, and finally, Sapphire hung up.

"You dropped me off at the airport," Sapphire said.

"Yeah, I did. But you wouldn't listen to me," Jamis said.

"I did listen to you and I didn't agree with you," Sapphire said.

"Can we agree that we disagree with what's happening and just wager who is right?"

"You have to be willing to accept that Levi might be responsible for what's happened," Sapphire said.

"And you have to be willing to accept he's not," Jamis said.

They sat in silence, watching people pass by them. Jamis stood to help a woman struggling with three kids and a cart of luggage. When she returned, Sapphire said, "I'll help but only because you just helped that woman."

"Whatever," Jamis said.

"You're not always right," Sapphire said.

"Neither are you," Jamis said.

"You have to buy me lunch and dinner," Sapphire said.

"Come on." Jamis stuck out her hand to pull Sapphire from the bench. "I'll carry your bags."

"I can carry my own bags," Sapphire said.

"If you come, you can't stay mad at me."

"I'll think about not being mad anymore after lunch," Sapphire said.

A truce descended upon them as they drove and Sapphire's hardened energy shifted as Jamis told her about the last encounter with Idana. They stopped at a drive-through, but Jamis wasn't hungry. Sapphire ate in silence after they agreed to talk to the woman who wrote her dissertation about Idana and made their way across Phoenix to the community college where she taught.

"The likelihood of learning about her from Baxter at the same time you did feels telling," Jamis said.

"Certainly, there is synchronicity," Sapphire said, still not as jubilant and open as usual. Jamis couldn't blame her. Their friendship was very new, and while they enjoyed kinship and mutual appreciation for each other's intelligence, the truth was they didn't know one another well. Time and experience were the only two factors that allowed humans to really understand and know each other. That and a willingness to trust that differences could be sorted out because each was invested in the same benevolent outcome.

But even that thought felt overly simplistic and idealistic. Maybe trusting others would always leave her feeling like she was perched on the edge of a cliff, just waiting for a strong enough wind to send her plummeting into the void. It was a depressing thought and it darkened her mood even more than it was before she fought with Sapphire.

"Are you ruminating?" They'd stopped at a stop light.

"Yes," Jamis said and turned to face Sapphire.

"About?"

"Trusting others and the void." Jamis turned away from her and put both hands on the steering wheel.

"Leaving me at the airport is shitty, but I could do more to listen to your intuition," Sapphire said. Jamis opened her mouth and Sapphire held up her finger. "This is a peace offering. Do not say anything to make it worse."

Jamis nodded, silently agreeing. After a few moments, her fear dissipated at Sapphire's willingness to listen to her feelings. All she'd ever wanted was to feel like someone heard her side and was willing to make adjustments. Something hard inside her shifted then and made room. For what she didn't know, but the space was there. Sapphire's willingness to forgive her and allow for her own role might have seemed simple to an outsider, but for Jamis, it was as revolutionary as Johnna's quiet acceptance.

Wanting to refocus on the current predicament, Jamis returned to Idana. "What is the name of the woman we're seeing?"

"Linda McDonald. Doctor, actually. She teaches history and women's studies," Sapphire said.

"She knows who I am? And still agreed to talk?"

Sapphire laughed. "Yes and yes. To be honest, she sounded almost eager."

They drove in silence, arriving at the community college about twenty minutes later. After a number of wrong interpretations of the campus map, they found Linda in her office with the door opened, waiting for them.

She wore her dark hair pulled back in a ponytail. Glasses obscured the color of her eyes, but not the tiredness Jamis sensed in them.

Sapphire introduced them and they took a seat across from her. Jamis was eager and ready to hear what she knew. They skipped all pleasant chitchat.

"I'm interested in Idana's journals and how you came across them," Jamis said.

Linda turned away and opened a filing cabinet behind her. The gears squeaked and the metal grated. She lifted a binder from it and set it on the desk in between Jamis and Sapphire. "This is a copy of it. The originals are stored at ASU's main library, in the archives."

"Can we make copies?" Jamis opened the binder and pulled it into her lap. The cursive was difficult to read, though the copy was good.

"You can take it," Linda said.

The answer surprised Jamis. "I mean, I'm happy to just go run this through a photocopy machine and bring it back to you."

"Honestly, I wish I'd never found them," she said and crossed her arms around her middle, as if to hold herself.

"Why?" Jamis handed the binder to Sapphire and leaned forward, elbows on the desk.

"She's a nightmare," Linda whispered.

"Tell me more," Jamis said.

Linda stood and shut the door into the office and returned to face them. "I'm an academic. I work in facts, with reason, evidence, peer reviewed conclusions, understand?" Jamis nodded. It was a big reason why she didn't become one. "If my colleagues found out what I'm going to tell you, well…" She trailed off, thinking.

"They'd think you were crazy," Sapphire said. Linda nodded. "Or worse. That you couldn't be trusted. Your conclusions couldn't be trusted. Your work would be invalidated."

"Exactly," Linda agreed.

"We promise not to tell," Sapphire said.

Linda looked at Jamis. "I don't want to be mentioned in any video you give, or any article that gets written about any of this."

"I promise," Jamis said and watched as Linda took off her glasses and wiped the corners of her eyes before putting them back on.

"When I ran across those journals at a consignment shop during grad school, I thought it was the jackpot. Actual, verifiable, journals of a woman and madam who'd been hung for shooting a man. It was going to be my epic case study of sex-based violence and how females have historically been disciplined harsher for violence against males than males against females. I made that copy of those journals that night, at a twenty-four-hour Kinko's. This was back in 1995. I finished reading them at three in the morning and I was so horrified and distraught about Idana's fate. I sensed anger in her journals, but not any malicious intent. Not then. I went to Jerome and met a man who dabbles in local history, interviewed him and learned about the myths surrounding her. He pointed me to an amateur historian—"

Jamis interrupted her. "Baxter?"

"Yeah. You met him?" Linda's surprise was obvious.

"Just earlier today, in Jerome. He told me about you, but couldn't remember your name," Jamis said.

"I took a ton of notes and came back home. That's when that final journal fell out of the bag I'd found." She reached to take the binder from Jamis and showed her a section at the back, marked with a tab. "After I read that, everything changed. I went to bed that night and woke up to find..." She fell into silence again. Someone dropped something in the hall behind them. There were voices and laughter. Silence descended and Linda spoke again.

"I woke to someone standing at the end of my bed. A man. He wore a hat and he said, over and over, 'She knows.' Then he'd disappear. It always seemed to happen around the same time, one in the morning. This happened for weeks. After my initial terror, I got interested, curious, and I tried to talk to him. If I turned on the light, he was gone. I was just dating my husband at the time, but he can confirm all of this." Linda paused and stared at her hands. She took a deep breath.

"Are you okay?" Sapphire shifted forward on her chair and put her hand in the middle of Linda's desk, as if she were considering reaching for her.

"I'm okay. Just gearing up for the next bit," Linda said. She paused for another moment and then continued. "But then, more disturbing things started happening. My cat disappeared. Just disappeared. She was an indoor cat with a lot of health issues. I found her at the pound, ready to be euthanized, and I swear, when I brought her home and cleaned her up, I heard a woman's laughter. Then, I started having vivid, lucid dreams about Jerome. I thought it was my deep dive into history, into the journals, and I went to see a psychiatrist. They put me on sleeping pills, to help, but that just made the dreams worse—"

"They can make dreams worse, sleeping meds and antipsychotics. It's a common side effect. I'm sure that's what they told you," Jamis said, interrupting again.

"Exactly," Linda said with relief and surprise. "That's exactly what they said. But the dreams just became more and more violent, chaotic. I got really sick. I went to the doctor and they said it was a sinus infection and they put me on antibiotics and steroids. But I just got sicker. My husband took me to the ER and they admitted me. Respiratory failure. My lungs filled with fluid. They still don't know why. I couldn't breathe. They intubated me. Some rare virus, they said. I was in an induced coma for three days, and during that time, I talked to this woman. It's all like a vague, shadowy dream now. But it's there, just at the edge of my consciousness. She's still here. Like a poltergeist, or something."

"Or demon, a succubus, a siren," Jamis said, thinking out loud, staring over Linda's shoulder.

"I'm so sorry that happened to you," Sapphire said and nudged Jamis with her elbow.

Startled from her reverie, Jamis agreed. "Oh, God, yeah. It's awful. You're okay now?" It hadn't occurred to her to offer Linda any emotional support. She was too interested in the story.

"Yes, thank you." Linda smiled.

"And the strange events?" Jamis opened the binder again.

"Gone as soon as I handed over the journals to ASU's library," Linda confirmed.

"Really?" It was Sapphire, head tilted, questioning.

"It's as if, well, her spirit was somehow attached to those words, and when I read them, I let her free. Or that's the sense I got when I woke from my coma," Linda said.

"I've heard of objects holding psychic power. Boxes. Necklaces. Items with tremendous emotional meaning. I mean, consider the Ark of the Covenant. The idea is that the meaning we assign to things somehow animates them," Jamis said.

"That's what I thought too," Linda said. Someone knocked on her door and she stood, indicating she'd be right back.

"Do you really think Idana's journals sent her to the hospital?" Sapphire took the binder from Jamis and closed the lid, hand on it.

"Maybe. I mean, it sounds pretty convincing. Just as convincing as a rare virus," Jamis said.

"I don't want to read these now." Sapphire stared at the binder.

"I think Linda somehow brought her back into existence when she read her words. Idana must have put a lot of herself in those pages. If she didn't transition after death, which we know is common when death is traumatic, then maybe she attached to those and when Linda brought them home, read them, felt them, and was empathic to them, it helped her undo the confusion about her death and state. Then, she just kept figuring it out from there," Jamis said.

"Wasn't there an episode of *Buffy* where a demon jumped into a computer from a book?" Sapphire held up her hand for Jamis to high-five.

Linda returned with a man who looked about her same age. He was tall and slim but Jamis didn't really pay attention to him.

"We think you read Idana back into consciousness, from the traumatized state she'd inhabited since her death." Jamis crossed her legs and put the binder back in her lap.

"It's as good a theory as any, but who is the old man? And this is my husband, by the way, Gabe Miles." Jamis and Sapphire waved. "I told him you were coming by. He wanted to meet you." After greetings, Linda opened the filing cabinet again. Jamis flinched at the grating noise. "Here. I forgot. This is a sketch of him." She handed Jamis a pencil drawing of the man who stood at the foot of her bed.

"Let's take a picture and send it to Charlie," Jamis said to Sapphire. It looked like the man she saw at the end of the hotel bed. The similarities were striking enough. Jamis hadn't really thought much about him, what with the serial killer on the loose. Sapphire took a photo and texted it to Charlie while they spoke. Jamis told Linda about Charlie, the house in the desert, the strange room, the fire, and almost forgot to tell her about the man in the hat and Levi. It was as if they were both fading from her mind.

"You keep forgetting about details?" Linda put her hands on the table, eyes wide. Jamis and Sapphire nodded. "That's what happened with me, while I read the journal. I'd read something, take notes, and then when I went back and read my notes, I couldn't remember writing it at all."

"It's like she enjoys obfuscation," Sapphire said.

"Playing with us. It's a game. It's fun for her. I'm not sure we need to derive any greater purpose from it than that," Jamis said. But she felt a chill run down the center of her spine and a sharp pain in her head above her eye. She rubbed it and squinted. There was more she should be asking. "What's in the journals?"

"The first ones are relatively benign. She was brilliant and an eloquent writer. She came West from Philadelphia, on her own. Her father was a working man who made enough to keep a roof overhead, but was violent. Mom died during childbirth. I sensed there was more but she didn't write it. I doubt women in those times necessarily had the words." Jamis shivered and clenched her jaw. Linda saw it and tried to reassure her. "But she survived. She began the journey on her own, as you'll read. She met her husband somewhere near St. Louis. She married him there and they kept moving West. Eventually, they ended up in Arizona, where he successfully obtained land and began running cattle, which brought him wealth. The tone turns darker as they settle more. According to her diaries, he had 'unnatural appetites' and she mostly tried to stay clear of them. They never had any children, but I inferred it was because of him, not her. Something 'off' with his parts, which she believed is what made him cruel. Day-to-day of life in the desert. The scorching heat. Loneliness. Ranch hands. The men who worked the ranch admired her. I sense they protected her, did what she asked. She helped her husband carry out business across the region, seemed shrewd. A visit north to Jerome where she fell in love with the views and town. The property he purchased there. Then, his death. His brother took the ranch. She negotiated control of the buildings in Jerome and moved up there, somehow. There are fewer entries at this point, likely because she was more occupied with living than writing."

Linda took a sip of water. Jamis imagined she'd be a great teacher.

"Is this too much?" Linda suddenly looked uncertain. Her husband shifted to lean against the wall right behind her and put his hand on her shoulder.

"No," Sapphire and Jamis said at the same time.

"Keep going. Please." Jamis fidgeted in the chair, getting more comfortable.

"But then, suddenly, around the mid to late 1890s, her tone shifts. She's angry. Vengeful. Thinking about causing harm. She's resentful about women's economic status. This is the time in United States history where women are earning rights to their own income and married women's property rights acts are taken up across the country. But Arizona didn't become a state until 1912. Even if her husband had left her the property, there was no state to protect or enforce her rights. Somehow, in some way, she felt cheated out of the ranch and its earnings. Something else happened in Jerome, around this time. You'll feel it. When you read it."

Jamis didn't need to read it. She felt it earlier in the day, in Jerome. But she didn't tell Linda that. "I can't thank you enough for sharing all of this with us."

"Of course. Please be careful. I don't think the photocopies have quite the same punch, but you never know."

There was something nagging at her consciousness, like a toddler tugging his mom's hand. An elusive thread of connection began to form, though she didn't know it then. It was just the first stiches in an elaborate tapestry of interconnectivity that would take her to the truth. "One more thing," Jamis said as she stood and moved her chair so Sapphire could get out. "Who else knows this story?"

"Just the two of us," Linda assured her.

"And it all really happened," her husband told them.

Jamis shook their hands, picked up the binder, and left the office as Sapphire chatted with them a few moments longer.

They took the stairs to leave the building. The movements of the day had caught up with her and Jamis wanted to eat and stare at the television, but a pressing compulsion, and concern for Levi pressed her forward. Sapphire grabbed her arm on the landing of the stairwell and showed her a Facebook photo of Linda and Gabe.

"They seem normal enough," she said, but there was hesitation in her voice.

"I find it disturbing how you stalk everyone on the internet immediately after meeting them," Jamis said.

"Don't judge me for who I am as a person," Sapphire said.

Jamis laughed. "There's something obvious I'm missing. I feel it right here," Jamis said, touching the space between her eyes.

"What is it?" Sapphire shifted her bag on her shoulder.

"I don't know."

"Thought you had some genius insight," Sapphire said as they slowed their pace.

"You might give me too much credit," Jamis said.

"Well, lets rest. Take a power nap. I want Mexican food. Not Del Taco. Like real stuff from a hole-in-the-wall," Sapphire said, ignoring her judgement.

"Point the way, boss." The insight settled into the center of Jamis's thoughts, cloistered, but her unconscious mind began to shine and refine it, even if her conscious mind was on salsa and tortilla chips.

CHAPTER FOURTEEN

They booked rooms at the first decent hotel they found. It wasn't far from the campus. Jamis enjoyed the quiet, unmoving solitude. Her nerves were frayed by the constant movement of the past few days. The bed was comfortable enough, and she turned to her side and pulled her knees up to her chest, with a pillow between them. Her sides still ached from the broken ribs a few months earlier. She rubbed them absentmindedly and stared at the wall.

Her lawyer called as soon as she settled. She'd spoken with Levi at the county jail and were awaiting his pretrial hearing in four days. He was distraught but okay and relieved Jamis believed his innocence. How she would prove it was unsettled. Her lawyer echoed the concern. Preliminary DNA reports placed Levi at the scenes of gruesome, grotesque murders. Jamis asked them to spare her the details of what happened, and she did.

She'd arrived to this point with Stephanie Gardner as well. An impasse where nothing added up. Somehow, as she pushed forward the path unfolded and the truth arrived. It almost killed her, but that felt like splitting hairs. There was Idana, a brilliant but vicious ghost, haunting her dreams and days, talking to her in many different ways. There was a man warning others of her arrival. There was a real-life serial killer leaving DNA behind that matched Levi's. None of it made any sense.

Her phone buzzed. It was Carmen, checking in. Making certain her presence wasn't required. Jamis assured her it wasn't. She wanted to send Sapphire home, too. Her vacation time was likely just about up. Jamis hoped it was sooner rather than later, though, so she didn't need to worry about her safety.

She'd set the binder on the table next to the door. For some reason, she'd not opened it yet. Linda's warning had jarred her, and before anything else happened, she just needed to rest and be. But its presence nagged at her, and when she closed her eyes to try to ignore it, Idana's laughter drove them open.

Unable to get the rest she needed, Jamis went to the sink and rinsed her face. She stripped out of her clothes and slipped on a pair of shorts and a sports bra. She left the room with just her card key. The sun was as brutally hot as ever but tolerable. Jamis wandered the grounds until she found the path to the pool. After a few failed attempts to open the gate without swiping the key, Jamis realized her error and let herself in. It was a lovely pool, with fountains and built-in hot tubs. She left her room key on a chair, plugged her nose, and jumped in the pool.

The water was as warm as a bath. She sunk to the bottom of the pool and opened her eyes. The lights on the sides of the pool were visible. Tiny currents of water formed around the fountains. She pushed up from the bottom and took a long gasp of air, shifting to float on her back. There was only one other person in the pool, at the other end of the long and expansive structure. The sky was brilliant blue, dotted with few clouds and scorched red and orange to the west. A plane heading to Sky Harbor left trails behind it.

She drifted toward the portion of the pool in shade. Her mind was quiet, despite the stress of the last few days. The absence of gravity gave her relief. Just being alive was its own work some days, moving in a world of dense matter. Her aching ribs relaxed. The experience of the pool felt like a gift. It'd been years since she'd gone swimming.

She grabbed the side of the pool with one hand to hold still and allowed her body and consciousness to inhabit the present moment. The roar of the water filled her ears with a sort of white noise that blocked out all the world. Jamis drifted from the present to somewhere else. The water disappeared. She was on land again, her body heavy with gravity.

Idana greeted her with a smile. "You're back and you have my journals."

"Where am I?"

"Same place in space, just different time," Idana explained.

"I was in a pool," Jamis said, turning around in a circle. She was surrounded by desert in all directions. There were buildings in the far distance, but they looked like a mirage.

"Yes, you were, and now you're not," Idana said and walked toward her. "You've grown up very well since I saw you last."

"In Jerome, around 2003 or 2004, I don't remember. I saw you didn't I?"

"Yes. I think maybe I saw you before," Idana said.

"Where?"

"With your mom, in California," Idana said, stepping closer to examine Jamis.

"Why would you be looking for me? I don't understand." Jamis took a step back.

"I won't hurt you," Idana said.

"I'm not so sure." Idana seemed to respect her need for boundaries and held still. She was as tall as Jamis. It was the first time she'd noticed.

"I've taken an interest in you for a long time. Took a while to get your attention," Idana said.

"Why's that?"

"Why's it taken time to get your attention? Something shifted in you recently. Opened up. Allowed me to connect," Idana said.

"No, I mean, why are you interested?" Though what she shared interested Jamis too.

"Isn't it obvious?" Idana tipped her head and smiled at her as she spoke.

"No," Jamis said.

"It will be," Idana said.

"Then just tell me now," Jamis said.

"Why would you believe me if I did?"

"You're scary, but so far, seem pretty honest, at least to me," Jamis said.

"It's true. I was always honest, even when I was in a human body like you," Idana said.

"How do we meet like this? This happened to me before, with someone else. This sort of interaction," Jamis said.

"Your ideas about consciousness are quite on point. The problem is that humans develop these lanes and then everyone has to drive within them. Those lanes blur human capacity to see beyond the bounds of what is defined. For some reason, we can. I died in human form but didn't want to migrate back into the whole. I'm rather attached to this unique consciousness," she said.

"So, you mean you and I shared this sort of talent for seeing outside the lanes of defined human consciousness?" A chill ran up her spine and light exploded in her head, twinkling like the stars in a far distant galaxy.

"Exactly. When we're human we know nothing about anything at all, but my goodness, do we like to think we do," Idana said.

"I like antibiotics though," Jamis said.

"I'm not sure what those are. But whatever they are, it's likely just another tool that lets humans believe they understand the fabric of reality," Idana said.

Jamis stared at her. "What do you want with me?"

"Isn't it obvious?"

"No," Jamis said.

"To teach you. I've been waiting for you," Idana said.

"Why?"

"You'll see. Better go now. You're floating in water," Idana said.

Jamis jerked back into her body and sunk downward, struggled to return to the surface, and coughed up water as she did. She wiped her face and hung on the side of the pool, arms crossed, head down.

Either she was on the cutting edge of consciousness or she needed stronger psychiatric medication.

She swam a few laps, her body falling into muscle memory. Idana wanted to teach her about human consciousness. Somehow, she'd figured out how to stay attached to the human world and inhabit the space between life and whatever came next. Whether there was any connection between her and the serial killer and vicious little demon she met in the desert was uncertain. Somehow it was all intermingled. Jamis sensed she should remain skeptical of Idana, even as she reached out her hand in companionship.

Jamis climbed from the pool, the sudden return of gravity heavy on her ribs. She grabbed her right side with her left hand, bent to pick up her room key, and shuffled back to her room, the peace from earlier gone. The cement sidewalk was hot under her feet so she picked up the pace. The cold air of her room made her shiver when she opened the door. She'd lost thirty minutes. Jamis looked at the times on her phone and the clock on the nightstand multiple times to confirm.

She stripped out of her wet clothes, hung them over the towel rack to dry, and rinsed off quickly before dressing again.

It was almost time to meet Sapphire for dinner. She'd try to get her to return to Utah and would wrap all this up by herself. Jamis was most comfortable that way, anyway. She texted Sapphire who responded immediately. They met outside.

"I went swimming," Jamis told her.

"I took a fifteen-minute nap and talked to Sam."

"I saw Idana again, while I was in the pool," Jamis said, and then told her the details of their encounter while driving to dinner at a restaurant Sapphire chose.

Once settled, orders placed, they resumed their analysis of the situation, until they were quieted by authentic Mexican food.

Jamis plowed through her plate of enchiladas and beans, drank three glasses of water, and two Diet Cokes before she felt satiated. "I was starving."

"It's your dimensional hopping. It always happens," Sapphire said.

"I want you to go home tomorrow," Jamis said. Sapphire looked as though she was going to argue, but Jamis held up her hands. "I insist. I'll be fine."

"I'm not leaving you alone," Sapphire said.

"I'll be fine," Jamis said.

"You're kidding, right? Remember last time you went off half-cocked? You almost got killed and Carmen had to save you."

"That was different," Jamis insisted.

"How?"

"Well, I didn't know that the killer was still in the wild. Now I do," Jamis said.

"That's stupid," Sapphire told her.

"No, it's not. And anyway, you think Levi is the killer and now he's in jail, so it's fine. I'm hunting for Idana's purpose for contacting me and that's it," Jamis said.

"You don't think Levi did it," Sapphire said.

"You were clear I was wrong, so you can't use that against me now."

Sapphire covered her head with her hands. "You make me crazy." It was muffled but Jamis heard it.

"Well, that's rude," she said.

❖

After dinner, Sapphire retreated to her room and Jamis called Johnna on FaceTime. She shared what she learned and held the binder up for her to see.

"So, what I hear is maybe Levi is guilty," Johnna said.

"Honestly, I just don't know," Jamis said.

"But you've hired a lawyer for him."

"I mean, it's my lawyer," Jamis said.

"They came from LA?"

"No, they're here, in Phoenix. I met her when I lived here, and then retained her when I got famous, you know," Jamis said with a grin.

"What is it about Levi? It sounds like you're projecting," Johnna said.

"How I've missed our psychoanalytical sessions," Jamis said.

"I'm serious though. He's sort of orphaned," Johnna said. From behind her, Jamis heard Sam.

"Say hi to Sam for me," Jamis said. Sam heard and called back to her. "Are you at his place?"

"Yeah. But back to projecting," Johnna said, challenging Jamis.

"I don't think he knows his dad, and his mom won't help him," Jamis said.

"Well, at least you see it," Johnna said.

"Maybe you missed your calling. You should have been a therapist," Jamis said.

"No. I don't like that many people. I just take a special interest in you," Johnna said. Jamis touched the screen with her finger. She missed her.

"Wanna read this journal with me. I mean, it might be demonic, or something," Jamis said.

"Like the demon thingy?" Johnna was struggling for context, but before Jamis could reply, she said, "I don't believe in such things. And if they are real, well, I've managed more than one feral cat, so I think we're okay." Jamis watched her. Her quiet and calm were not to be mistaken for weakness, because at times, Jamis was sure she was the stronger of them both.

"Okay, here we go," Jamis said. If it invoked a demon, brought Idana back to life, made her manifest in the physical, in the middle of the room, no one could say she didn't warn them. Jamis fell silent, reading. After a few moments, she said, "Idana was a really good writer, at a time when women's literacy was not a priority."

"An articulate and literate poltergeist feels kinda scary," Johnna said. Jamis agreed with a slight nod, still reading. Something about Idana shook her foundations and made her feel unmoored. Idana was seductive, but she wasn't seducing her. She was terrifying but wasn't mean to Jamis. She was elusive but seemed to want to open up. On some level, Jamis felt like once she crossed that bridge, nothing would be the same.

"I think those words are what give her power," Jamis said.

"What do you mean?"

"Well, it's just that she didn't seem to exist here, in this dimension, until her journals were read," Jamis said.

"You realize that sounds..." Johnna paused.

"Unbelievable?" Johnna nodded. "It's true I think. When we write, we pour ourselves into our words," Jamis said.

"Certainly a journal would evoke a lot of emotion. Or a story, drawn from personal experience, told from our heart would hold a lot of the person writing it," Johnna said.

"Sure. Our lived experiences captured in words, immortalized in print, is a piece of you," Jamis said.

"Well, you said that Idana seems interested in you. Not necessarily scary to you—"

Jamis interrupted. "Oh, no, she's scary. Like eating people alive scary, and she takes over my emotions and makes me think about doing awful things."

"What's the answer then?" Johnna tipped her head, questioning. Jamis watched the now familiar mannerism on the small screen of her phone. "Do we read or do you come home? Let your attorney sort out Levi?"

This was what Jamis needed. She'd been running in place. Not getting anywhere. She needed clear choices and a clear direction. Johnna was always clear about the choices in front of her. She had the capacity to take all the noise and simplify it. It was because she was always so present. Jamis hadn't been since arriving in Phoenix. Anxiety was preoccupation with the future, depression the past. She heard her psychiatrist's words in her head. What was her objective? Johnna had just given her the choice, not that there ever really was one. But that she could choose it consciously meant everything could be different going forward.

"We read," Jamis said.

"I thought so," Johnna said.

CHAPTER FIFTEEN

Okay, this is from June 1866," Jamis said. "'I've fled Philadelphia hidden in the far back corner of a train compartment. It is hard to see and write, but I intend to continue my record of my life, as I began it when I was young.' The writing is so bumpy, like she couldn't keep steady," Jamis said.

"Let me see," Johnna said, so Jamis angled the phone camera to point to the paper. She started reading again.

"'I lost those journals when I left father's house tonight. I brought only a few dresses, the money I took from his study, and a few of my favorite books. I intend to travel west, where I've heard women can secure their own land.'"

"She was bold," Johnna said.

"I'm telling you. She's scary as hell, but likeable," Jamis said and flipped the pages in the binder, looking forward. "I'm gonna skip ahead. Her husband died in 1885."

She stopped on a page dated February 1885. "So, there is a big gap between, let's see. She wrote in December 1872, a few every year going forward, stopping in 1880, but not again until this one, in February 1885," Jamis said and then continued to read.

"'It is nothing but wind and sun. Days pass and I have no idea how to orient myself. Every direction I turn looks the same, and often, I see things I should not. Tempered by my desire to have more for myself, of myself, I've taken necessary steps to liberate myself from this situation. I shall not confess any ill action, but only good fortune in my husband's untimely death. In Philadelphia, consumption, cholera, typhoid, and many other ailments plagued the living. Out here, violent death is the more present threat. It is, if I am honest, what I've hoped for. A violent death for Ned, not at my hand, so I might go on. He fell last night, from high, the boards of the ladder splitting under his weight. His thighbone cracked as he fell. The men said they heard the snap. Not a few hours later, he left the world convulsing before the doctor could even be summoned. Now my issue is his brother. He may have this godforsaken place, should I retain the buildings in Jerome.'"

"Did she just say she killed her husband? Like, by weakening the boards?" Johnna asked.

"Maybe. She told me he had some unsavory sexual impulses and that the room out there was his," Jamis said.

"She told you?" Jamis held up her hands in a dramatic shrug gesture. "I assume this happened in an episode."

"Is that what we're calling them now? Episodes," Jamis said with a grin.

"For lack of a better word at the moment," Johnna said. A loud bang on the door startled them. "What was that?"

Jamis jumped from the bed, phone in hand, and looked out the window. "It's just Sapphire." She opened the door.

Sapphire rushed in, laptop in hand, face excited and frantic. "You have to call your lawyer."

"What? Why?" Was she being arrested? Were the cops on the way?

"Because Levi did not kill anyone," Sapphire said.

"I told you," Jamis said.

Sapphire took a deep breath and flapped her hands in front of her and then closed her eyes, calming. "Okay, okay. So I decided to try and look at the police files—"

Johnna cut her off. "I'm sorry. Did you just say you hacked the police files?"

Sapphire shrugged and looked at Jamis, who said nothing. "Oh, is Johnna on the phone?"

Jamis nodded and Sapphire answered her question. "Hi. I mean, yeah. It's what we do."

"Sapphire," Johnna said, a note of caution in her voice. Jamis stood the phone up on the table so Johnna could see them both.

"I mean, we take liberally from rent seekers and the police state," Jamis said.

Sapphire pointed at her. "What she said. So, anyway. I got in there and they've arrested him on preliminary DNA evidence. But get this, when I dug deeper, they know the DNA doesn't really point to him. It just points to someone who is related to him. Like a father or a brother. I'm not quite a DNA expert, but it's just a relative match, and they have to know that."

"You mean he's not guilty," Jamis said, now on her feet.

"No, at least not based on this evidence. They're retesting the samples because they think there is a mistake, but I'm almost sure there isn't," Sapphire said.

"I'll call my lawyer," Jamis said.

"No, don't." It was Johnna. Even virtually, Jamis knew she was deep in thought. "Because you'll need to explain how you know and you can't. So, just wait. Levi is safe. Your attorney is in touch with him. Just slow down. The question is, if it's not him, who is it, and how is it related to anything the two of you have gotten involved with," Johnna said.

"You're suggesting that we allow the justice system to run its course," Sapphire said, tone a little indignant.

"Yes, I am," Johnna said.

"For a young male, person of color?" Sapphire raised her eyebrow. "Because that works out so well, so often."

"I'm not suggesting we don't intervene. I'm just suggesting we don't act rashly. How will you explain how you've gotten this information? What we should do is have Jamis's lawyer request that their expert review the DNA evidence as part of discovery, which she's already likely to do, once they get there. It will sort itself out without you implicating yourself in a multitude of state and federal crimes," Johnna said.

Sapphire and Jamis stared at Johnna on the phone and then looked at each other, conceding to her perspective. It was sound and wise. "Are you going to argue with me?" Johnna wanted to know, voice firm.

"No," Jamis said hesitantly, and Sapphire nodded.

"Good. In the meantime, you need to understand the connection between Idana, these murders, your current course, and Levi," Johnna said.

Jamis held up her hands in surrender. "I have no fucking idea. But you're hot when you're bossy." Johnna laughed and Sapphire whistled.

"With that, I'm going to let you two go and finish up with Sam. I see him struggling behind me," Johnna said.

"Don't struggle," Sapphire called with panic in her voice. From behind Johnna, Sam's voice filtered to them.

"I'm okay. But I could use her help," he said.

Jamis smiled and blew Johnna a kiss, who returned the gesture and hung up.

"She's amazing," Jamis said.

"Dude," Sapphire said in agreement.

Her phone rang. It was a 520 area code and a number Jamis didn't recognize.

She answered on speaker. "Jamis, it's Baxter."

"Baxter, hi. Tell me you thought of something else," Jamis said.

"Yes. Crimes against humanity," he said.

"Right. That's why she was hanged. For murder and crimes against humanity," Sapphire said.

"You're on speaker. That was Sapphire. Go ahead," Jamis told him.

"She likely had a child out of wedlock," he said.

"What? How does that relate to crimes against humanity? There had to be something else," Jamis said.

"No. That was a crime against humanity then. Check the journals. I think she had a child out of wedlock. And likely, wanted to keep him," Baxter said.

"How do you know it's a him?" Sapphire stared at the phone as she asked the question, deep in thought.

"I don't know. Just using him as a default," Baxter said.

"Presumptuous pronoun usage," Sapphire said.

"Probably not relevant," Jamis whispered.

"It's always relevant," Sapphire said. Jamis winked at her.

"Idana was a mother? And she was hanged for it?" Jamis couldn't quite believe it.

"I'm guessing. I've been thinking about it off and on since I saw you, and women could be tried for crimes against humanity for getting pregnant out of wedlock, and I just think maybe she did," Baxter said.

"But why? Couldn't it be something else? Like robbery, prostitution, or something else she dished out during her illustrious career as town madam?" Jamis was unconvinced. Baxter was silent. It occurred to her that she didn't believe him because he wasn't telling her something. "What aren't you telling me?"

"Nothing. I have to go." He hung up the phone. Jamis stared at it, screen now dark.

Sapphire took the binder and scanned the pages, one by one. "I don't see anything about a child, unless it's in code," Sapphire said. A few minutes passed. "About what year would this have happened?"

"She was born in 1852, so any time after up until when? How late can a woman realistically get pregnant? And then, during that time, I think we'd have to adjust for healthcare, carrying to term, and such," Jamis said, thinking out loud.

"And why would it matter?" Sapphire was engaged completely with the thought, no longer distracted by Levi's DNA. Johnna's arguments had prevailed.

"It could be motivation," Jamis said.

"What do you mean?" Sapphire asked, but didn't look up from the journal.

"To hang on after death, to commit murder, for all kinds of things," Jamis said. A committed mother was the fiercest foe in nature.

Sapphire closed the journal and opened her mouth to speak when another knock on the door shocked them all. Jamis pushed back the drapes and peered outside. "It's the police."

Sapphire dropped the binder, opened the laptop, and tapped quickly. "Hold on," she said, almost frantic. About thirty seconds passed and another pound shook the door. Sapphire shoved the laptop in between the mattress and box springs. Jamis helped her.

"Police. Open up," the shout echoed.

Jamis yanked open the door. It was Andrew, Vera, and two plainclothes officers. "Was that really necessary?"

Vera pushed into the room, looked at Sapphire. "Why is it always you two?"

"What are you talking about?" Jamis put her hands up, innocence and confusion real.

"I got a phone call from an anonymous source that identified the two of you as Levi's accessories in murder. The person told me you were here and were holding someone hostage and likely accessing police data illegally. Then, about forty minutes ago, our server was taken down for two minutes, and when we brought it back up, a huge chunk of data had been downloaded," she said.

"Well, that's just awful," Jamis said.

"You know anything about it?" The look on Vera's face told Jamis she already knew the answer.

"How could I? I've been here, with Sapphire, my best friend, all afternoon," Jamis said.

Vera looked at Sapphire. "I know who you are. And your internet reputation."

"Who? Me?" Sapphire pointed at herself.

"Just because nothing has stuck before, don't think it won't this time," Vera said.

"Stuck what? I'm sure I have no idea what you're talking about. I'm an archivist for a small town in Utah, for God's sake," Sapphire said.

"And a known Antifa sympathizer," Andrew said.

"Now that's just too far," Jamis said. The detectives turned to her. "I mean, she's an idealistic, Bernie loving Democratic socialist, but she's not Antifa. Pretty sure that's fake news." Sapphire smiled at Jamis's defense of her.

Vera told the plainclothes officers, "We've got this. You can go." Vera closed the door behind them.

"Sure, you can come in," Jamis said.

"Thanks, I will," Vera said as she sat in the chair at the small table by the window. She stared at Sapphire and Jamis and then rubbed her eyes. "I am so tired. I've been up for three days. Every time I think I can go home and sleep, something else happens. And Andrew smells and needs to shower." He nodded and leaned against the dresser.

"I'm sorry to hear that," Jamis said. Why were they there? Was their relaxing with them a ploy to entrap them?

"No, you're not. But it doesn't matter. What does matter is that every lead takes me back to the two of you. The explosion in the desert. The body in Jerome. Levi. This phone call and anonymous tip. The hack of our servers. I want you to be totally honest with me, no ghost stories. No bullshit," Vera said.

"I told you what I know. And I've told you about Idana Drake. That's her diary right there." Jamis told her about Baxter, Linda, and Idana's communication with her.

Vera rested her head on the table. "I give up." She stayed that way for a few minutes and then sat. "Okay, so here's what we're going to do. Andrew is going to go home, see his wife and kids, shower, and sleep because I can't stand him anymore. I'm going to stay with you and see what happens next."

"I mean, I really don't know what I'm doing next," Jamis said.

"My mother loves your show. Used to make me watch it with her. I'm sure you'll figure it out," Vera said.

❖

"Well, this is awkward," Sapphire said, still sitting in the middle of the bed.

"This is what it's come to," Vera said.

"I just don't think this is necessary," Sapphire said.

"Where's your laptop?" Vera pursed her lips, challenging her.

"Didn't bring it," Sapphire said with a shrug.

"You're lying," Vera said.

"I mean, what you're doing is illegal," Jamis said.

"How so?" Vera turned to face her.

"You can't just stay with us until something happens," Jamis said.

"I don't know what else to do," Vera said.

"Well, that's your problem," Jamis told her. They glared at each other. Was Vera a big ol' lesbian too? Jamis thought she might be. Should she ask? "Okay. Let's figure this out. We can help each other," Jamis said, signaling a potential truce.

"You tell me the truth," Vera said.

"I can show you," Jamis said.

"I'm listening," Vera said.

"Let's sleep tonight and go to the desert and Jerome tomorrow. I've got Idana's diary. I'm going to read it. Levi told me he was supposed to take me somewhere. So you bring him too. You know he's not guilty by now, right? That DNA was just preliminary and you overreacted." Jamis took a chance. Vera bit her tongue and sighed but didn't argue. "You come with us tomorrow to Jerome, and we'll go from there."

"What's the point of it though? What comes from that?"

"Answers," Jamis said.

"You don't even know what questions you're asking," Vera insisted.

"Listen, you came to me because of an anonymous tip. I didn't come to you. I mean, who called you? Don't you want to know? I think it's the maniac behind all of this. I've only told you the truth. And despite your disbelief, you've not arrested me, or her." Jamis pointed at Sapphire. "And I think you need our help."

Vera covered her face with her hands, and they sat in silence for five minutes. Finally, she spoke. "Fine. I'm willing to try it. God knows why but I am. But first, I want to see this diary, and I want to go over what happened in the desert one more time."

"You look really awful," Jamis said. Vera stared tiredly at her.

CHAPTER SIXTEEN

Vera left after another round of disbelieving questions about what Jamis saw in the desert. Jamis urged her to call Detective Pete in Utah so he could vouch for her. Vera said she'd consider it. Sapphire waited quietly on the bed for a few moments after Vera left and then dug between the mattresses to find her laptop.

"Can they know it's you?" Jamis pointed, worried about her.

"No, they can't," Sapphire said.

"But are you sure?"

"I've hacked every major government institution in the world. When I was a teenager, and definitely Antifa," Sapphire said with a grin.

"Fake news," Jamis said and hugged her.

"I'm going to bed," Sapphire said.

"I'm so tired," Jamis said.

Sapphire shuffled out the door. Jamis listened for the door to open and close and hit the wall a few times. Sapphire responded with one loud smack on the wall so she latched the door and fell onto the bed.

She fell asleep fast, the nonstop movement of the day wearing down her active mind. The air conditioner was set at sixty-five degrees so at some point in the night, she shifted under the covers. Soundless, dreamless sleep carried her into oblivion.

She woke as sun filtered into the room. Her phone said it was five, but she felt rested and clear minded.

Jamis readied for the day and texted Sapphire. When she responded, Jamis found coffee and continental breakfast for them in the hotel lobby and delivered them to Sapphire's door. Vera and Andrew were there, waiting for her.

"Morning, sunshine," Andrew said.

"Gonna have to get your own coffee," Jamis said. She knocked on Sapphire's door with her elbow. Sapphire opened it, eyes bright, obviously refreshed as well. Jamis held out the coffee and donuts.

"Cops are here," Sapphire said. She waved all of them into her room.

"So, let's hear the plan," Vera said.

"How's Levi?" Jamis woke determined to see him freed from jail.

"Order to release him is moving through channels. He'll be out this afternoon," Andrew said.

"Don't you feel guilty?" Sapphire's eyes hardened and flashed with anger. Her passion for justice was inexhaustible.

"No. The DNA match was preliminary and we made a best-case judgment call. If it had been him, we had a responsibility to the public," Vera said.

Sapphire opened her mouth to speak, but Jamis cut her off. "Fine. Let's go out to the desert. There's something there I didn't get to and it's been nagging me."

"The ranch house you blew up?" Vera was texting as she spoke and it annoyed Jamis.

"I didn't blow it up, your serial killer did," Jamis said.

"We'll drive," Vera said.

"Fine by me. Save me mileage," Jamis said, briefly wondering about the status of her scorched rental car.

❖

The ride to the desert was longer than Jamis remembered from their first day. Likely, the route from central Phoenix was longer than the path they traveled from the airport. Sapphire insisted they stop at Del Taco so she could eat, and Jamis joined her inside at a booth while Andrew and Vera ate outside in the car. Their dynamic felt uncomfortable but not confrontational. Pete had texted that Vera called him, so Jamis assumed that had helped her suspicions.

When they finally arrived, Jamis's heart raced with the same dread she felt upon her first arrival and her instinct was to jump from the back of the moving car and run as far away, as fast as she could.

Andrew stopped the car and Sapphire leapt from it, obviously relieved to be free from the confines of it with them. Jamis followed her. The house was still there, but someone had pulled the RV away. Only indentations showed it was ever there. Poor Charlie and Gwen. The strange cellar room was opened and excavated. Jamis stood at its edge. Iron and blackened, charred wood remained. Nothing else.

"That's where we found the body," Vera told her, now at her side.

"Why did it explode though?"

"Propane. The homeowner used it to store propane. The perp likely didn't see it there," she said.

Jamis left the site and wandered around the house. Some of the frame was charred, but it could be salvaged. She thought it was much worse when it happened. The RV took the brunt of the explosion. Something pressed against her shoulders. She shook her arms, not wanting to engage with the entity that had tripped her up before.

She was there because something about the property kept nagging at her. The man in the hat appeared then. Jamis met his eyes and walked to him. He took off his hat, but his features were not in focus. He walked away from Jamis toward the back corner of the property. Jamis followed him, steps deliberate and measured. He was taking her to the wall that called to her during her visit before. There was nothing significant about it. It was just blocks, fixed together with mortar, the lone standing remnant of a building someone cared enough to assemble at some point.

She breathed deeply and wanted to retain the calm she awakened with so she could see clearly. From the corner of her eye, she saw Sapphire begin to follow her. That was fine. She'd not resist support. The block wall was coming into focus. Once again, she was struck by the sensation that there was something behind it. She'd done this before though and found nothing. What did she expect to happen this time?

A few steps from the wall, the air shifted around her, cooling. She saw her breath and shivered. The light changed. From summer to winter, she thought. The sun seemed softer. She kept walking. Something charged from behind her, wrapped its arms around her neck, and screamed in her ear.

"You've come back, Jamis," it said, but she ignored it, walking forward. "Did you come to see what we've been up to all these years out here, Jamis?"

She didn't respond. She sensed that fear gave it power. "Did you know that the reptile came before the bird, and the bird before the mammal?" That made her stop. What the hell was it talking about? "Oh, Jamis is interested in evolution," it said, voice crackling.

"Is that what you are? What came before the reptile?" Jamis engaged, too interested not to. Its long blades were dangling down the front of her. When it spoke, there was warm breath on her neck.

"You're so wise, Jamis. I'm what came before what came before the reptile," it said.

"Why do you just hang out here? Why not see the world? Make some friends?"

"This is where the door is. That lets me move between all the worlds I like to visit," it said.

It was an interdimensional being. Nothing in Earth's biology books. Jamis didn't say anything else because she'd arrived at the wall. The man in the hat turned the corner, and when Jamis stepped behind him, he was gone.

She ignored the pressure of the creature on her back and circled the wall. After her second trip around, she felt a slight variation in her step. She wouldn't have noticed it during her last visit because there was so much going on.

She paused, backtracked, and stepped again. There it was. She looked down at her feet. When she looked back up, she was surrounded. At least twenty hungry ghosts swarmed her, screaming for their retribution. Jamis felt the fury of their denied justice and gulped for air. One of them grabbed Jamis's shoulders and cried into her face. Half of her scalp was missing. Another grabbed her hand and yanked her toward him, frantic.

"My daughter. Where's my daughter?" he cried, asking her the same question again and again. All of them cried out with their last thoughts. The trauma of their deaths left them stuck in the moment it happened. A large man with a beard and in overalls cried for his mom, and bloody tears ran down his face. She was overwhelmed and so closed her eyes and fell to her knees.

She felt the ground with her hands and dug, piling the dirt next to her. By the time Sapphire arrived to help her, Jamis had unearthed a wooden hatch with an iron handle.

"I knew there was something here," Jamis said to Sapphire and moved to open the door.

"How?" Sapphire put her hand on Jamis's and said, "Wait."

Jamis looked up at her and nodded, but as soon as Sapphire left, she yanked the handle. It screeched open and the entity on her flickered away, squealing with delight. A putrid smell slammed into her, and she fell back, gagging. She crawled away on hands and knees, frantic to escape it. Vera and Andrew rounded the corner of the wall just as Jamis fell backward and both cried out, arms over their mouths and noses.

"I told you to wait," Sapphire yelled.

Jamis scrambled farther away and stood, hands in the air in a shrug. "I think I just found more bodies," Jamis said.

❖

Vera and Andrew called for backup and the site swarmed with officers and forensic teams. Jamis sipped a Diet Coke and sat next to Sapphire on a stoop leading into the house. The wind picked up again and she was desperate for some sort of shelter. Based on the varying states of decomposing bodies, Vera and Andrew realized neither Jamis, Sapphire, nor Levi had anything to do with the murders.

Vera told them some of the bodies were practically mummified, which was likely a result of the dry desert air and cellar they were stored in.

"How did you know?" Sapphire didn't make eye contact as she asked the question. Instead, she twirled the tab of the pop can on her fingers.

"The guy in the hat that everyone keeps seeing. He showed me. And then that demon thing tried to keep me from it, I think," Jamis said.

"He took you there?"

"Yeah, it's crazy," Jamis said. Then she told her about the other souls bound to the spot. Sapphire was quiet for a while.

"I'm relieved. There's no way they can blame Levi now. Some of these bodies have been there longer than he's been alive," Sapphire said. Jamis agreed and took out her phone to text Johnna and Carmen. Tell them what was happening. "But who is doing it? And why?"

"That I don't know," Jamis said.

"I feel like we're closing in though," Sapphire said.

"Should I finish reading Idana's journals?" She didn't want to. Something kept her from rushing forward. A deep hesitancy told her to take it slow.

"No," Sapphire said immediately.

"Just checking," Jamis said.

"I think it's possible this has been happening for a really long time," Sapphire said.

"The creature told me there are doors here, that let it move from world to world," Jamis said.

"Right," Sapphire said, expression pinched.

"What? You don't believe me," Jamis said.

"I wish I didn't. You're not hearing doubt. You're hearing a hefty dose of terror mixed with existential angst," Sapphire said.

"Because we're ants in a complex universe we don't understand," Jamis said.

"Right," Sapphire said and closed her eyes.

Vera asked a patrol officer to take them back into Phoenix around noon. Jamis and Sapphire were both grateful. Vera's demeanor had changed and she approached Jamis with caution and curiosity.

"I don't know how I do it or what it means," Jamis said.

"What?" Vera stared at her, waiting for context.

"You're wondering how all of this happened, and I don't know," Jamis said.

"It's got to be tiring," Vera said. Jamis waved at her and climbed into the back seat of the police car. Sapphire was in the front, tapping on her phone, likely texting with Sam.

"You should go home tomorrow," Jamis said. Sapphire ignored her.

Jamis fell asleep, once again dreamless and sound. She opened her eyes at Sapphire calling her name.

"Come on. We're at the hotel," Sapphire said, standing outside the car. Jamis joined her and thanked the officer for the ride. "You were out."

"I slept like a log last night too," Jamis said. "I need ice and water. Some food. They have a snack bar."

"Yeah, let's run to the lobby and regroup. Figure out what's next," Sapphire said. They watched the police car drive away and walked slowly on the sidewalk, their mood mellowed and muted from the events of the day. All of those people, dead, under such horrible circumstances. Jamis was drained by the onslaught of emotion she'd experienced finding the cellar.

The water splashed from the fountains into the pool. Laughter and what sounded like a cannonball into the pool took over the silence. Jamis wondered if she could summon Idana at will. If there was an unused spiritual mechanism for placing a long-distance call between the living and the dead. She had no idea how to conduct a séance, though she'd pretended to participate in numerous ones during her show's tenure. She really just needed Idana to tell her what was going on.

She pushed her fingers through her hair. Her clothing felt sticky and sweaty. She shifted her shorts in an attempt to be more comfortable as she moved. The lobby doors were within sight. Sapphire's phone rang.

"Take it. I'll meet you in there," Jamis said. Sapphire stepped into the shade of a hallway in route. It was probably Sam. They'd regroup. That's all they needed to do. But just as she turned the corner of the path to enter the lobby, something pinched her neck, and the edges of her vision dimmed, and all she could say was, "Not again."

CHAPTER SEVENTEEN

"Jamis, wake up." It was dark. It felt like her eyes were open, but she couldn't be sure. She tried to lift her hand to touch her face, but it felt heavy, as if she were drugged. The pinch in her neck. She managed to get her fingers to her collarbone, and then up the skin of her neck. There was a small bump. Did someone stick her with a needle? "Jamis." Jamis stuck out her hands, touched the ground, and tried to stand. Her legs wobbled. "Jamis, it's Sapphire. Someone grabbed us outside the hotel."

"Where are you? Tell me what way to turn. My eyes feel weird," Jamis said. They burned, and as she rubbed them, her vision blurred.

"They'll acclimate. Give it a minute. He must have given you more," Sapphire said.

"What do you mean?" The edges of the room began to take shape. There was a small window above her, rectangular and small. Specks of moonlight filtered into the darkness. She followed the path of the light to Sapphire's silhouette. "I can see you now."

Sapphire came toward her and took her hand. "I don't know where we are. I couldn't find a door."

"There has to be a door," Jamis said. She started in the corner closest to her and walked the perimeter of the room, hands touching the wall, looking from cracks. She found one, opposite the small window. "It's here." The handle had been removed and the edge sanded. Sapphire joined her. "See if you can get your fingers in there and find the latch." Jamis felt for the hinges, but they were likely facing the opposite direction. She stopped and leaned against the door, sliding down to sit, suddenly exhausted.

Sapphire joined her, their shoulders touching. "Do you think it was that guy from the desert?"

"Obviously," Jamis said, appreciating that Sapphire didn't call him a serial killer out loud.

"Well, we're trapped," Sapphire said. Jamis rested her head on her knees, pulled up tight against her chest. "I wonder how long we've been missing."

It was a good question and gave her something productive to focus on. It was almost three when they got to the hotel. She'd looked at her phone right before Sapphire left to take a phone call. Would the cops realize something happened to them? How long until Johnna realized something was wrong? Jamis imagined her fright and regretted causing it. She should have gotten on a plane when all this started to unravel and just let it go. Not only had she risked her own life, she'd risked Sapphire's.

Sapphire moved and blocked some of the light from the window. "Can you tell what time it is?"

"Can I or is it reasonably possible?" Jamis asked and pushed up to her feet to follow her. Jamis stood on her tiptoes to look out the window. "Is there something to stand on?"

"It's empty. Nothing here," Sapphire said.

"Step in my hand. Like in the movies," Jamis said. She bent and held her hands together for Sapphire.

"You're kidding," Sapphire said.

"Come on, tiny tot," Jamis said, and Sapphire made a noise in between a cry and laugh. She stepped into Jamis's hands, gasped as she was pushed upward, grabbed the window ledge, and looked out.

"We're out of the city, for sure, but I don't know where. The sun is setting, but just barely," Sapphire said.

"Been at least a few hours or so," Jamis said.

"At least. Lift me a bit more, if you can," Sapphire said. Jamis strained, arms starting to tremor. "I see a paved road, just off to the right."

"What? I can't hold you for much longer," Jamis said. Her arms started to buckle so she leaned against the wall to stabilize them.

"I just don't know where we are," Sapphire said. She pounded on the window, but Jamis could no longer hold her and they stumbled together across the floor. Jamis caught her before she fell.

A sharp bang sounded on the door hidden in the wall. It rattled and expanded, the thuds loud and consistent. The pounding grew in intensity and a cloud of red uncurled from the top of the door. It was the vicious little creature Jamis saw in the desert. It balanced on its tail, flashing its awful, yellow toothed grin before unfurling back over the top of the door, reverting to smoke. The pounding stopped.

"Did you see that?" Sapphire tugged Jamis's arm, pointing.

"Yeah, but you did too, so that's new," Jamis said. The pounding resumed and then, in the corner of the room, the man in the hat appeared. Jamis approached him, tugging to get Sapphire to release her grip. "Who are you? Why do you do this? You took me to those bodies."

The man stared behind her, the same phrase repeating, barely a whisper, again and again. "She knows. She knows."

"Right. She knows, but who are you?" The man's eyes were milky white, clouded with death. His skin translucent. Upon closer inspection, his pants hung baggy on sallow skin and a slender, hungry frame. He turned his stare to Jamis abruptly, and she stumbled backward to get away. He stepped toward her and took off his hat.

"She knows," he said, staring at Jamis.

"What does she know? Is it Idana? Who knows what?" Jamis yelled at him, exasperated by all the dead ends this path took her on. She was on an aimless mission, now prisoner of a psychopath, for what? A ghost with limited vocabulary? There was no one to redeem. No one to set free. Just an endless bombardment of terror, confusion, and darkness.

"That they're going to hang her. She knows. You have to go," he said.

"Idana knows they're going to hang her?" He flickered out of existence, returned to whatever space kept him between worlds.

"Who are you talking to?" Sapphire stood behind her, arms folded across her middle.

"The man in a hat, from the drawings. You didn't see him, I take it," Jamis said.

"No, but I saw a waft of red earlier. Where are we? We have to get out of here," Sapphire said.

"Can you fit through the window?" Jamis looked from the door to the window, and guessed it was their best bet.

"I might be able to. Just barely though," Sapphire said.

"I don't think I can," Jamis said.

"If they didn't want us to escape, wouldn't they have blocked that?" Sapphire paused, questioning.

"Maybe they didn't think it was big enough," Jamis said.

"What should I do if I get out? I don't know where we are," Sapphire said.

Jamis took a deep breath, calmed, and centered. Their location was isolated. There were crickets in the background and a faint coyote howl. Farther still were the sound of engines on a roadway. If Sapphire could get out, she'd be able to follow the sounds to the road and flag down help.

"Do you hear the cars? Just quiet and listen." Jamis took Sapphire's hand in an effort to calm her.

"Yes," she said. Jamis pushed her toward the window.

"Let me boost you. You get out, run for help," Jamis said.

"I can't leave you," Sapphire said. Jamis ignored her, turning to face the window to hoist her up.

"If one of us doesn't get help, we're both dead. I'll be okay. Find us help," Jamis said.

She felt Sapphire's hesitation. The deep intake of breath as she considered their options. There was no point trying to force the issue. Sapphire would do what she wanted to do. After a few moments, she spoke. "Lift me up, and for God's sake, don't die before I can get back to you."

Then, her foot was in Jamis's hand and Sapphire grasped the windowsill. "I'm sorry I left you at the airport," Jamis said.

"I'm sorry I didn't listen about Levi," Sapphire said, looking down. She wiggled the old handle on the window and pushed it open. It began to squeak. She stopped, hesitating.

"Just do it fast," Jamis said. She cranked the handle, the squeal loud and unmistakable as grinding metal. With the window opened, she crawled up, her body half in and half out. "Push," she said in a loud whisper and Jamis complied. She grabbed Sapphire's feet and pushed upward.

Sapphire disappeared and then stuck her head in the window. "Stay alive," she said.

"Go, before they see you," Jamis said. She grabbed the window, stood on her tiptoes and saw Sapphire disappear into the dark of the desert. They had no phones or GPS. There was nothing outside to help her know where she was. Their only hope was that Sapphire found the road before their captor found her.

Jamis pulled the window closed and sat, legs in front of her, tired and weary. Once Sapphire got to town, they'd send help. They couldn't be too far from the hotel or from the city. She just didn't think enough time had passed.

She closed her eyes, focused on her heartbeat, and heard steps outside the door. The pounding began again and she covered her ears with her hands and tears ran down her cheeks. She became aware of pain in her knee. She touched her right knee, and her hand came away covered in blood. She'd not noticed it before. The pounding continued, but Jamis faded away from it, instead focusing on her body, making an inventory of injuries. Knee. Left elbow. Stinging eyes. Her pinkie on her left hand was swollen.

Despite the noise outside the door, Jamis's small personal bubble was quiet and calm. It was a skill she honed during her turbulent younger years. She would just pretend it wasn't happening. Even if her body betrayed her terror and shook. The sound of a door handle turning returned her to the present, and she scrambled to her feet to hide in the corner on the same wall as the door. She was obscured by darkness.

The door opened but no light came with it. It was as dark outside, which felt like some sort of advantage to her. There was no movement, no shadow. Jamis resisted the urge to rush the open door. After a few minutes of standoff, the person on the other side of the door stepped into the room. His large figure loomed in the door, visible enough to confirm it was the man from the desert. Jamis clenched her fists and wished she could will herself through the wall.

"You can't hide, you know," he said and turned on a flashlight. The beam filled the small room and landed on her. Jamis raised her middle fingers at him as it did. "Where's your friend?"

"Beats me," Jamis said. He rushed around the room, frantic, and then looked up at the window.

"That's too small for anyone to get out," he said. He easily reached the window. "And it was stuck shut. God damnit." His fury was palpable and Jamis shivered as she felt it. He rushed to her, grabbed her by the arm, and yanked her forward into the middle of the room.

"Oh my God, I am so sick of men doing that," Jamis yelled and struck at him, connecting her fist to the top of his head. She squared up, ready for a fight. He fumbled the flashlight and just enough of it lit up his face. Jamis stepped forward as he struggled to recover. It was Linda's husband. He stood right next to her in the office as she listened to his wife talk about Idana. His appearance was so brief and inconsequential the idea would have never occurred to her. He was in the same room with her, just the day before, acting the doting husband. What was his name? "Gabe."

He dropped the flashlight and stared at her. His hat was askew and he adjusted it.

"Anyone ever tell you your red hat looks like a MAGA hat?" Jamis took a step back. "Why are you doing this? Have you killed all those other people?"

"Yes," he said, posture relaxing. It was like he was relieved to be recognized.

"For Idana?" Jamis didn't understand the connection.

"Idana made me realize who I really am. They're a gift for her. When my wife found her diaries, we found each other," he said.

"Does she tell you who to kill?"

"No, I do that on my own." He took a step to Jamis. "Except you. She told me to bring you here. I tried getting Levi to do that, with my friend you've met."

"The demon thing?" Jamis took a step back, hands almost on the wall.

"Suppose. More of a companion Idana introduced me to," he said.

"Like a puppy," Jamis said, now against the wall. There was nowhere else to go. There was something familiar about him. The way he moved his head when he spoke. His long arms and legs. She was missing something obvious. She needed to keep him talking.

"All those people. In that hole in the desert. Why did you use the new one? Cause that explosion? You had a good thing going," Jamis said.

"Not all of those were mine. I learned from someone before me. He lived out there, until he got sick," Gabe said.

"But you met him because your wife found Idana's diaries?"

"Magical, isn't it? And you met me because Charlie and Gwen got that place from Jessica. She knew you know. What her husband was. What he did," Gabe said.

"Charlie and Gwen's aunt knew her husband was a serial killer?" It was too much to take in. The chain of events that brought them to this point, stretching back decades. Those bodies, sealed up under the earth, their souls trapped and restless.

"Of course she did. It's that place. The energy from other worlds bleed through. Stain us. It was the perfect place for Idana, she just couldn't get there," Gabe explained.

"She's dead. Why can't she get there? I think mobility is easier when you're dead," Jamis said.

"Not when you've been banished. All those years ago. She can only circle. But all those souls could sustain her, if she could just get to them," he said.

"I have no idea what you're talking about," Jamis said.

"Most people don't understand," he said.

"But I'm not most people." Idana couldn't get back to the ranch she lost to her husband's brother because she'd been banished. Trapped souls were there. "Why did you come out there that night to leave that person? Was it the first time?"

"There, yes. She told me to. To find you. To start all this," Gabe said.

"So you expected me to show up at your wife's work. You called the cops on me and Sapphire when we got to the hotel. You followed us from there," Jamis said.

"You showing up there was a surprise. When she called me at work to tell me Jamis Bachman, the famous ghost hunter, was coming to visit her, it was a dream come true," he said.

"Glad to be a crowd pleaser," Jamis said.

"She said I don't get to kill you, so don't worry. But since your friend got out, we are going to have to go somewhere else." He lunged and grabbed Jamis. She was slow from earlier, sore and shocked. He had the rag over her nose and mouth before she could protest. She dug at his hands and arms, skin peeling up under her fingertips. She struggled against the rising unconsciousness and her last thought before she faded was, "This is Levi's father."

Bumps in the road jostled Jamis from side to side. Her hands were bound behind her back. It was dark and hot where she was. She tried to sit up, but her head struck metal. Panicked, she thrashed, trying to get free. Her head was fuzzy and vision blurry. A sharp bump told her she was in the trunk of a car. Her eyes adjusted. Wires for taillights were just visible. She calmed and listened as the car accelerated. There were other cars. Sweat ran into her eyes and burned. She closed them for relief. The sounds of the car engine were blatant, and she heard it turn over to climb in elevation. The transmission pulled. She was going back to Jerome and imagined they were somewhere on I-17.

She was so tired. The past few days were an onslaught of nonstop activity. Something was injected into her neck and the effects of it lingered. Whatever had sent her into unconsciousness during her struggle with Gabe had cleared. But her body was heavy with chemical fatigue, which was a familiar sensation because she'd taken pain pills for a few weeks after her last bout with a psychopath.

Her arms throbbed. Would crying help? Should she just sob, get it all out, and come back to the situation with a fresh frame of mind? There was such a desperate feeling in the spot below her breastbone. It radiated down to her root chakra and then traveled into her legs. Would it even be possible for Sapphire to find her now? Or would she just die, her body mutilated, burned, and left for Vera to find? How would Johnna go on, knowing how she died? She'd already experienced such traumatic loss. It wasn't fair.

Jamis centered her focus on the feeling of despair and ignored the tingling in her limbs. She accepted her plight and surrendered to the idea of her upcoming death completely. She would die and all she could hope was that it happened quickly. When she opened her eyes, she expected to see the inside of the trunk. Instead, her view was magnificent. The sun was rising above the hills. A crisp, cool breeze chilled her, and she gripped her own upper arms for warmth.

"I've always loved this view," Idana said, suddenly next to her.

"A poltergeist with deep appreciation for nature," Jamis said.

"Is that what you think I am? A poltergeist?"

"I suppose. In the absence of any other word," Jamis said.

"What if I'm evolved? The next step in evolution. An anomaly the universe will be certain to try to repeat," Idana said.

"I find that disconcerting," Jamis said.

"Well, that is rude," Idana said. There was the unmistakable sound of horses galloping. The thud echoed in the early morning air. Jamis turned toward the sound, searching. "That's for me," Idana said.

"What is?" Jamis faced her again, questioning.

"Gareth Hamilton, don't you remember? He's coming to hang me," Idana said.

"Are you showing me things in some sort of order? Should this make more sense to me?" Jamis shook her arms at her sides. They tingled. It was probably some sort of strange sensation bleed through from reality where she was bound in a trunk of a car.

"I'm trying, but it's hard to maintain a linear hold on things from this side of things," Idana said.

"Why did you kill that guy? I don't remember his name," Jamis said.

"Jacob Monihan. He was my lover you know," Idana said.

"No, I didn't." Jamis said nothing else.

"He betrayed my trust," Idana said.

"So you killed him?" Jamis stared at her, braced for the answer. When Idana didn't respond, Jamis said, "Like you killed your husband by weakening the boards in the ladder."

"You're reading into things," Idana said. But she smiled and her eyes glimmered with amusement. The horses drew closer. "Don't be alarmed when they hang me. We do this again and again. It's what I'm trying to stop. It's why you're here."

"To help you not get hanged?"

"Yes. I think we can share enough of an emotional charge that I can disrupt this cycle," Idana said.

"I don't understand," Jamis said.

"You will. Just stay with me. Don't go anywhere. When we're done, I have so much to teach you," Idana said. She straightened her hair, adjusted her skirt and top, and pulled the dark black veil down over her face.

"Did you dress this way on the day you died?" Jamis, without thinking, adjusted her veil where it was curled up on the side. Then she wiped some dirt from her sleeve.

"Thank you, Jamis," Idana said.

"Sure," Jamis said, hands dropping awkwardly to her side. Why did she do that? And with such tenderness and care?

"I'm not a poltergeist," Idana said.

"I'm getting that," Jamis said.

"I'm really just here, stuck in this loop, gathering strength," Idana said.

"How are you stuck in a loop?" Jamis asked the question but didn't expect an answer. Idana didn't give her one but turned away and strode toward the galloping horses ridden by at least a dozen men. Four jumped down and rushed Idana, grabbing her arms.

As they spun her, she said, "Don't try to interfere."

"Who are you talking to? What are you doing?" The tall man, obviously the leader, grabbed her shoulders and demanded an answer.

"It's none of your concern, Gareth," Idana said and winked at Jamis. "When you've been killed as many times as me, the shock sort of wears off."

"You've not died yet," Gareth said.

"I'm not talking to you," Idana said, but then she grew quiet and closed her eyes. They bound her hands and walked her to a tree. One of the men threw a rope over it and tied a noose which was fastened around her neck. They hoisted her up on the horse and positioned her under the branch. Jamis watched, in shock, and yelled when someone smacked the horse's hind end. It jerked and charged forward and Idana swung. Jamis screamed, involuntarily, and rushed to try to grab her legs. She fell right through her. Despite having touched her before, she was intangible now. Jamis cried as the life drained from Idana's body and shook from the trauma. She avoided looking at her face and ran away, but the desert background gave way to empty blackness and Jamis plummeted.

It felt as though she fell for hours, but then, as suddenly as the drop happened, Jamis was back on the dusty road, standing next to Idana, just as she was before.

"My God," Jamis said, alarmed.

"It's not pleasant, but I've grown used to it. Now we have a bit more time," Idana said.

"Why are you doing this to me? Why did you have someone kidnap me?"

"Because you're special," Idana said.

"No, I'm really not," Jamis said. Somewhere, a bird squawked. Her eyes burned and arms tingled again. The ground felt unsteady under her feet.

"You're special to me. And I think you're the key to helping me get free. Your emotional charge is what I need," Idana said.

"I'm highly rational," Jamis said.

"Well, that's still emotion. You think you're so certain of who you are and what you're doing, but you have no idea yet. You will though," Idana said.

"I can't help you at all if I get killed," Jamis said.

"I won't let you," Idana said, hand on her arm. Then she kissed her cheek and was gone. Jamis closed her eyes and opened them again as the lid of the trunk opened. She saw only a flash of a figure before a bag was over her head. Gabe yanked her from the trunk of the car and she stood on wobbly, uncertain legs. He pulled her forward, grip painful on her arm. Light filtered through the bag on her head telling her the sun had come up. Would anyone ever find her?

A door squeaked open. She stumbled up stairs and stepped more tentatively going forward. Her mouth was dry and she needed something to drink and eat. She took sixty steps before he pushed her into a room. He shoved her back and she fell into a chair. He cut the ties around her hands, but before she had a chance to move or resist, he bound them to the arms of the chair. Jamis couldn't move them anyway. Having them bound behind her back cut off her blood flow and she couldn't feel them to move them.

He yanked the bag from over her head. Bright sunlight filtered into the room through cracks and broken windows. She had to be in the old school Blaire and Devon had taken them to investigate. Gabe left the room and Jamis tried to even her breathing and wet her mouth. She shook from the drugs and shock of her experience, her legs trembling.

Gabe returned with a bottle of water he unscrewed and held up for her to drink. Jamis hesitated, but then he poured water into his own mouth, to demonstrate its safety. When he returned it to Jamis's mouth, she drank hungrily. He unwrapped a bar of some sort and fed her pieces before offering her another bottle of water. It was a strange development, but it helped Jamis recover some of her strength. Her eyes still stung. Her thoughts were still fuzzy, but the water and nutrients made her think survival might be possible. That may have been the point, just to string her along, make her hope when there really was none.

CHAPTER EIGHTEEN

Jamis really didn't know how much time had passed except to guess as she watched the sun move in the windows. It was unbearably hot, and she drifted in and out of sleep. Her dreams were anxious and uneasy. In one, she chased after Johnna who kept running, not stopping even when she called her name. In another, Stephanie Gardner was back, head gashed open, screaming for her justice. She cried out for Emma, for help, and no one came.

Ice cold water across her face was what jolted her awake at some point. The sun was disappearing in the west and she'd lost track of all sense of time. Gabe dumped a gallon jug of water on her head and then offered her a bottle to drink. She'd lost all concern for poison or drugs. He fed her another bar and it tasted like chalk in her mouth.

"More water," she mumbled and he actually complied. Jamis closed her eyes, the relief of hydration bringing her back out of where she'd retreated in her mind. Her lips were chapped and burned. Gabe stared at her and she lifted her gaze to meet his. "What?" She asked him the simple question with a direct challenge.

"You'll see," he said and left the room again. A few moments later, he returned with Blaire and Devon, both bound and gagged.

"No," Jamis yelled at him, a surge of adrenaline seizing her. Her surrender and resignation were replaced with fury and indignation.

"Yes," he said and pushed them forward, gun in his hand. He forced them to sit back to back. He wrapped a rope around their ankles and then tied it to opened doors on either side of the room. He put the gun in the waistband of his pants and took out a sharpened knife. He nicked Jamis's cheek with the tip of his blade and laughed when she flinched. Warm blood spilled down her cheek.

"Ouch," he said.

"Don't you dare hurt them," Jamis said and tried to move her ankles, but she was bound so tight the rope wouldn't budge. Why hadn't she tried to escape earlier in the day? Since when did she just give up?

"Wrong," he said. He grabbed the door Devon's feet were tied to and slammed it shut. Devon screamed out in pain as he was yanked forward. Jamis assumed the loud snapping noise was his leg bones. She shuddered, tears involuntary. How much trauma could one person take on?

"Leave them alone," Jamis screamed, trying to stand. She thought she could take the chair with her, but it was bolted down. Devon sobbed, calling for his mom. Blaire cried silently, her strange eyes opened wide in terror. "Why are they even here?"

"Oh, I invited the idiots. First, I paid them to get you here. When they failed that, I told them to meet me here tonight for a special ghost hunt," he said, kneeling next to Devon. He rubbed his head and laughed at his pain. Then he turned quickly, kicking out at Blaire. He connected to some part of her because she screamed with pain.

He came back to Jamis. He held her chin in his hands. "She told me to make you angry enough to kill me."

"You're doing a great job," Jamis said. Devon stopped crying, likely because he'd passed out from the pain. But she heard Blaire's sobs. "They're just kids." They'd only come because they idolized her. She'd put them at risk and their lives and pain were her responsibility. "If you let them go, I promise I'll try to kill you."

"I like to take my time anyway. It's why I always burn them after. Clean up my mess," he said.

"Not enough. They found your DNA," Jamis said.

He turned, shocked. "What?"

"Yeah, only they thought it was your son. They didn't have yours on file," she said. That was the connection. This was Levi's father. The how and why she could sort out later. The pieces all snapped together, falling into place. Levi moved just like him.

"I didn't leave anything," he said.

"Well, you must be getting sloppy because they've found DNA on the last two victims. And Levi is in jail for it." How would Levi feel learning this monster was his father?

"We could really influence him, you know." Jamis assumed he was talking about his demon-pet and Idana. "Because he's mine. I've watched him for years. His mother was a mistake and so was he, but I was interested. When he became a cop, I thought it might be useful. Idana told me to use him to get you here," he said.

"She really put all this in motion?" If she kept him talking, maybe he'd leave Blaire and Devon alone.

"She's a master strategist," he said. Jamis was angry. Everything from the email until now was orchestrated. Jamis felt adrift and lost because she wasn't charting her own course. Idana was. What she wanted with her, Jamis still didn't know.

"Do you know what she wants from me? Other than to make me angry enough that I want to kill you," Jamis said.

He stared at her, as if deciding whether to answer her. "Don't think I've forgotten about your friend," he said and left the room, muttering to himself.

The guy was just a garden variety psychopath who felt important because Idana talked to him and gave him instructions. There was nothing more to it than that. She wondered why Idana had a vested interest in his butchery. What was she getting from it? Jamis understood him at least, but Idana remained a mystery. What did she hope to gain from Jamis's participation?

"Blaire," Jamis said.

"Yeah," she said, tone soft.

"How long have you been here?"

"A while. We were out there for a bit, but I don't know how long," Blaire said.

Jamis hoped Emma was watching. That she'd reach through dimensions and untie her hands like last time. But she didn't. Instead, the knots grew tighter the more she struggled against them. In a moment of insight, Jamis relaxed her whole body and the tension from the ropes eased. Her skin burned where they'd rubbed her raw. The bolt holding the right front leg of the chair looked loose, so she casually rocked back to the left, hoping to loosen it more. It wiggled and hope surged in her.

She increased her pace and it popped free. Doing so loosened the other bolts and she stopped just long enough to capture her balance. She perched forward and slipped the rope around her ankle under the leg of the chair. She repeated it on the other side. Her hands were still bound but her legs were free.

When Gabe returned to the room, he lit a dozen candles with a striker and then left again, to return holding a long metal tool that looked like a fire poker, and moved toward the door that anchored Blaire. Jamis knew there was no waiting. She lunged upward and collided with him, shoulder in his midsection. He dropped the rod and the knife anchored to his belt fell off. Jamis threw herself on the ground in an attempt to break the chair but it didn't work like it did in the movies. She managed to break the left arm of the chair so she could slide her arm out of the rope. She scrambled toward the knife with her right arm bound painfully to the chair.

She grabbed at it, but it spun from her fingers as he kicked it. He grabbed her arm and twisted it painfully behind her back. Jamis screamed and kicked him in the kneecap. He stumbled and fell backward, losing his footing. Somehow, Blaire had managed to free herself and was there, in front of her. She cut the rope free from Jamis's arm and scrambled behind her, toward Devon, as Gabe charged again.

Jamis picked up a candle and flung the wax in his face. He screamed and clawed at it. Jamis picked up the stone block propping the door open and struck his head. He dropped, unconscious. Jamis finished pulling the ropes from her hands and helped Blaire untie Devon. A bone stuck out of his leg and Jamis averted her gaze, unable to tolerate the sight. Blaire struggled to help him stand. Finally, Jamis pushed her out of the way and tossed him over her shoulder, like a sack of potatoes. She didn't know where the strength came from.

She thought about taking the time to tie up Gabe, but decided it was more important to get to their car outside. They left the well-lit room and plunged into darkness. They were somewhere in the heart of the old school, and every step felt treacherous. It was condemned for good reason. Jamis stayed close to the wall, wishing she had something to light their way. Blaire abruptly left and returned a few moments later, with a candle.

"Well done," Jamis told her. Devon's weight was becoming problematic. The surge of adrenaline that propelled her earlier was dissipating and she was beginning to feel the physical toll of everything that had happened. Blaire moved in front of her, cautiously guiding them through the hallways. To the right, a door opened into another room and the fading light of dusk helped them. Jamis could see the vague impression of an outer wall and what looked like a hole in the ceiling.

"Just ahead," she told Blaire, who acknowledged her with a brief nod. Something crashed behind them. The echo of whatever it was filled the space. Then, there were footfalls.

Thump. Thump. Thump. Each step sounded like a drum beat. Jamis knew it wasn't Gabe, but that didn't make her feel any better. The *thump* sound increased its pace, as though its owner were running toward them. The door they passed slammed shut and behind them, a scream momentarily drowned out everything else. The man in a hat was back, watching from a distance.

Blaire screamed when she saw him, but Jamis used her free hand to push her forward. Whatever was behind them was worse than him. *Thump. Thump.* A figure in white materialized to the left and Blaire stopped moving again, frozen.

"Ignore everything. Just get outside," she said and Blaire, to her credit, listened. Jamis was going to drop Devon. Her shoulder and ribs screamed in pain. The weight of him was too much. She just had to clear the open room and get them outside the school. That was her only thought.

They were out of the hallway and into the foyer Jamis recognized from their last visit. Fresh air filtered in from the open ceiling. Blaire pushed the front door open and stumbled down the broken steps. Jamis took them more tentatively, not wanting to let Devon drop until they reached their Hummer. Blaire yanked open the back door and Jamis threw Devon in the back seat.

"Where are the keys?" Jamis shook her arms, relieved to be outside. The sounds of the building receded behind them. The door to the school was open, and from the depth of the dark hall they'd just traveled, Gabe followed. He'd be on them in moments.

"We keep a spare set here," Blaire said, fumbling near the rear tire.

"Hurry," Jamis said.

"I've just about got it," Blaire said, holding a black box.

"Go," Jamis said, pushing her up into the car. "Go."

Blaire looked confused but listened. Jamis left her and ran toward Gabe, hoping to give them a chance to escape.

"No, we can go together," Blaire yelled from inside the car. But Jamis ignored her and leaped on Gabe as he came out of the school, arms around his neck.

"Get out of here," Jamis yelled. He tried to pull her with him to the car, but Jamis dropped her feet and held on to him, struggling to maintain her balance. Blaire started the vehicle and sped off, dust flying. Jamis and Gabe struggled, arms and legs flailing, but she was losing the battle. Her body was slow and sluggish from the drugs, previous injuries, and carrying Devon. Just as she resigned herself to her fate, something knocked Gabe from her. Jamis fell back and landed hard, legs outstretched. Gabe fell too, hard on his side, and grabbed his middle like the wind was knocked out of him.

Jamis covered her face, exhausted. It was too much. She just wanted to go home. She wanted Johnna. How many of these situations could one person reasonably expect to survive?

Idana materialized, blew Jamis a kiss, and disappeared.

Idana had given her a chance to get free of Gabe. She summoned all her will to stand and run. After sitting all day long, her muscles were slow to respond. She stayed close to the road, hoping someone would see her and help. The muscle just below her shoulder blade cramped and she almost fell over. She had to keep moving, no matter how tired she was. From behind, she heard his footsteps and labored breathing.

Jamis was not in shape. She didn't run like Johnna or lift weights like Sapphire. She walked when she could, but otherwise enjoyed her sedentary life. In this moment, she regretted not caring more about exercise. Her legs burned and eventually, gave out. The exertion was just too much. She crawled toward a large saguaro and hid behind it, hoping it was too dark to see her tracks. Gabe rounded the corner, pace even, like he jogged for fun. Jamis quietly took a long gasp of air.

She held perfectly still as he ran by. She didn't let out her breath until he was no longer visible. Jamis closed her eyes against tears again. Someone had to be coming to help her. But how would they find her? The cramping in her muscles grew and she rubbed her legs with her hands. How did Johnna run miles every day? Who did this to themselves voluntarily?

Jamis crawled away from the saguaro, farther off the path. She managed to rise to a half standing position, legs shaking, and headed toward the road again. Gabe had stopped and she could see him ahead of her, scanning the horizon, not looking in her direction. There were car lights in the distance.

Gabe saw them too. He looked at them for a few moments and took a flashlight from his pocket. The beam of the light was wide and bright and Jamis dropped to the ground to avoid it. But she wasn't fast enough. He saw her and came in her direction. Quickly calculating her options, she knew her only way out was the car heading her way. Jamis ran to it, waving her arms, hoping whoever it was would see her and help her.

While she ran toward the car, Gabe ran at her. Whether she'd make it to the car first or not was the gamble of her life. Somewhere, a surge of strength and will powered her final steps and she pulled ahead of him. Did she imagine the cheers of a crowd like they were at the Kentucky Derby? Idana was back then, materialized for just a moment, off to the right. Her laughter filled the night. What did she want with her? Gabe seemed to stumble. He was just visible in Jamis's peripheral vision.

The car was going too fast. If she didn't make it to the road before they made the turn to the old school, they'd miss her. She wanted to yell out for help, but her voice was caught behind her exertion. Tears flowed freely down her cheeks. She didn't want to die, and the absurdity of her situation wasn't lost on her. She was a ghost hunter. She had no business being chased by living humans. It was becoming a trend and it needed to stop.

Who was in the car? Her legs became lighter as she approached the road. She waved her arms wildly as the car raced by her. It skidded to a halt, brakes squealing, and the passenger door flew open. It was Levi.

"Levi," Jamis yelled. He ran to her, put his arms around her, and she collapsed against him. A shot rang out, and they both jumped backward. Dr. Baxter Clemson stood in front of the car with a shotgun pinned against his shoulder. Gabe stumbled toward them, in the middle of the road, and Baxter pulled the trigger again. The shot was deafening and Jamis covered her ears. Levi did the same. Gabe fell forward, hands outstretched, face contorted in fear and pain.

Torrential rain began to fall. Large drops of rain splattered on the dry earth. Idana materialized to her right and shifted into a transparent version of herself. Jamis slipped through time with her again. They were in the same spot, only it was foggy. A man was running from Idana. It was the man from her vision, all those years before. Idana consumed him and then folded back into herself, blinking out of existence.

"Did you see that? That's the lady from my dream," Levi cried, pointing. Levi had slipped in time with her. Or they'd both seen a projection from Idana's consciousness she wanted them to see.

"She's a soul eater," Jamis said, new understanding organizing itself inside her. "We just watched her eat that guy. I don't think we can trust a soul eater." Which meant her friendliness to Jamis could turn in a moment.

"Isn't she divine?" Baxter dropped the shotgun as he asked the question. His demeanor changed. The amiable doctor of transpersonal psychology became harder, darker, and more intense. He approached Jamis and Levi, holding the gun by the barrel.

"You're kidding me," Jamis said as she realized Baxter was also involved with Idana.

"Imagine my great surprise when Levi, newly released from prison, showed up at my house, frantic to find you," Baxter said.

Levi stepped in front of Jamis, shielding her from Baxter. "I didn't know. I swear I didn't. We split up to find you. They let me out and the cop gave me a ride to my truck in impound. He told me you were missing. That the DNA wasn't mine."

"I know. It was his," Jamis said, and pointed at Gabe.

"But how—" Levi tried to speak, but Jamis interrupted him.

"He's your dad. Your biological father," Jamis said.

"What? I mean, I don't understand," Levi said.

"I know it's a lot right now, so let's talk about it when we get rid of Baxter here," Jamis said, new strength emerging as she realized Gabe was neutralized.

"Don't be so cavalier. First, we have some unfinished business," Baxter said.

"No, we don't. We're going to get in the car and go," Jamis said, moving to the open car door. Baxter held up the shotgun. "You already took two shots."

"Modified gun clip," Baxter said.

"Maybe I do hate our gun laws," Jamis said.

"Spoken like a true Californian," Baxter said, clearly enjoying a return to their original banter. Jamis wasn't though and was frantically trying to find a way out. "There's no point. She's been waiting for you and I have everything ready. So let's go, both of you." He held the shotgun up and pointed it at Levi's midsection. "You drive. You in the passenger seat," he said to Jamis.

They complied. There was nothing else to do. All she could hope was that Blaire and Devon would reach help and it would narrow down the search for them. Levi put the car in drive, careful to avoid Gabe's body, and turned them around in the dirt patch in front of the old school.

"Is Sapphire okay? I sent her for help," Jamis said to Levi.

"Yeah, she got a ride into town. You were just out in Carefree, just north of Phoenix," Levi said.

"So Vera and Andrew know? I didn't know—"

Baxter interrupted Jamis. "That's enough," Baxter warned her, gun pointed at them.

"What does it hurt for us to talk?" Jamis turned to face him, suddenly and inexplicably fearless. "I've been drugged, abducted, tied up, and chased. Just in the last twenty-four hours. If we go back further, I can expand my résumé of experience with assholes like you." Unexpectedly, surprising even herself, she leapt over the seat and grabbed at the gun. They struggled for control of it and it went off, blowing a hole in the top of the car. The sound was deafening, and Jamis and Levi both covered their ears.

"Do that again and I'll blow his head off," Baxter yelled, spit on his lips as he spoke. There was perspiration on his forehead and Jamis pointed at it. He wiped his forehead with a forearm.

"Just saying for someone so cool, you seem to sweat a lot," Jamis said and turned back around, arms folded.

"Turn right up here," Baxter said, ignoring her. Levi complied and followed his other directions. It was a short ride and Levi stopped the car in front of a black wrought iron gate into a cemetery. Even the swirl of the metal was foreboding. Nothing good was coming. "Take your hands off the wheel, open the car door, and get out. If you run, I will shoot you."

Jamis could barely hear him because her eardrums were ringing. Levi opened the driver's door and they climbed out at the same time. Baxter followed, gun in Jamis's back.

"Big gun, tiny man," Jamis said to Levi and Baxter jammed her.

"You're not going to rattle me," he said. Jamis stopped walking, despite the pressure of the gun in her back. The view was what Idana had shown her when she was locked in the trunk. The tree where she was hanged was still there, but it had been cut down to a trunk and a few dead limbs. Jamis turned in a circle and noted the headstones and small monuments. From her vantage point, she could see all of Jerome. She left Baxter, despite his insistences and strode to the tree. She faced the same direction Idana did as she died.

Baxter and Levi faded from her awareness. Her stomach grumbled and her legs trembled from exhaustion, but she ignored it. Instead, she called for Idana who appeared, next to her, in her black dress again.

"You wanted me here. So tell me why," Jamis said.

"But first," Idana said and grabbed Jamis's arm.

"Jamis," Levi yelled and she turned to watch him rushing toward her, arms outstretched. But then he was gone, as was Baxter and the world she knew. The valley in front of her was full of motion. Heavy mining equipment dotted the visual landscape. Men strode purposefully around it and into the mines. The smell in the air was putrid. Chimneys burned with smoke. Idana took her hand.

"Let me show you my world, so you understand," she said and they moved, as if they were transported, and now stood inside the brothel where Jamis had lunch just a day or two before.

CHAPTER NINETEEN

Idana looked a little younger, less tired. Something about her complexion glowed.

"I'd only been here for a year or two," Idana said, next to Jamis, who was shocked to see her twice.

"How…" Jamis tried to figure out how to ask the question but was unable so let it go.

"I'm sharing my memories with you," Idana said.

"Like a telepathy," Jamis said. Certainly she'd heard of such possibilities. There were documented instances where people were able to communicate over long distances. Like a child calling a parent for help.

"Yes, so now that we've given it a name, can we continue?" Jamis waved her hand as if to agree. "I was happy during this time. It was the first time in my life I'd felt that way," Idana told her.

"I can understand that feeling," Jamis said.

"Yes, it's like you are now, with Johnna," Idana said. Hearing Johnna's name come out of Idana's mouth made Jamis cringe. If Idana noticed, she didn't seem to care. "This is when I was seeing Jacob. I knew it'd never be a marriage. I didn't want to be married. I just wanted my life here, my freedom, my power."

"Is power important to you?" Jamis followed Idana as they walked through the building, pausing to look at gas lamps and oil paintings. It was hot and dusty and Jamis wondered how anyone lived in it full time.

"It's important to everyone. Without it, you're nothing. Subject to being cast about by other people's whims and desires," Idana said. Jamis agreed with that too. She'd worked hard for her financial independence and personal power. She did what she wanted, when she wanted. But she didn't tell Idana this. She didn't want to create an inappropriate sense of similarity that might be misleading.

Idana took them up the stairs to the room Jamis had seen before. The red-and-black wallpaper was unique and looked newer than in the vision before. Red-and-black tapestries also hung around the bed but were drawn back and tied. It was daytime when they walked into the room, but as Jamis studied it, it changed to night and the sounds of day were replaced with a woman's cries.

It was Idana, on the bed, giving birth. She was also by Jamis's side. "That was my child with Jacob," Idana said.

"Is this the high crimes? I don't understand why you'd be put to death for that," Jamis said.

"Having a child out of wedlock was punishable as high crimes against humanity. I had Jacob's son, a bastard," Idana said.

"What happened to him?"

"I didn't tell Jacob. I had him and sent him down to Phoenix. I wasn't capable of caring for him, but it didn't mean I didn't care," Idana said.

"Why did you shoot Jacob?"

"Because he found out. I still don't know how. And came at me, threatened me. Was going to get my child. So I shot him," Idana said, her tone even and calm.

"Did he want his son?"

"He did. He only had girls with his wife. Men and their offspring," Idana said.

"Why didn't you just tell him when he was born?"

"Because I didn't want to," Idana said. Jamis waited for more explanation, but nothing was forthcoming.

"Why are you showing me this moment?" Jamis moved closer to the bed and watched Idana hold the infant she'd just delivered. Idana looked at him, with tenderness but not affection, kissed his forehead and then shoved him into the arms of the woman standing next to the bedside. An oil lamp flickered off and someone replaced the light with a candle.

"Take him to Phoenix," she told the woman.

"Are you sure?" The woman was older than her, thick around the middle, with graying hair. Her face and hands were worn, but her eyes were soft and kind. A man came to her side and put his arm around her shoulders and smiled down at the infant, reaching a large finger out to touch his forehead. The infant wailed and the woman held him closer.

"Yes," Idana said and turned away, slouching down in the bed. Jamis moved out of the couple's way and followed them out of the room. Idana, her guide, followed as well. The couple picked up bags waiting at the bottom of the stairs. The woman climbed into the back of the wagon and the man into the seat, where he whistled to the horses. Jamis watched as they faded from view.

"Wait. You're still in the bed, how can we see this? This isn't part of your memory," Jamis said.

"Maybe it's part of the genetic memory of my child," Idana said.

It was night outside. Shouts and laughter filtered out of lit saloons. Drunk men straggled out swinging doors. The wagon with Idana's son was gone. The moment was surreal. Old Jerome. A dead woman who shared her consciousness with Jamis. Genetic memory, whatever that was.

"I'm not sure I understand," Jamis said, attention returning to Idana.

"Sure you do. Do you know who those people are?"

"I assume they're a kind couple who worked for you and couldn't have kids. It's like an after-school special," Jamis said, agitated and suddenly tired. A compulsion to leave overtook her and she wanted to be done with this conversation and memory. "Just take me somewhere else."

"See, you're trying to avoid it," Idana said.

"I'm not avoiding anything," Jamis said. She left and walked down the middle of Main Street. Idana stayed with her for a half a block before grabbing her arm again and turning Jamis to face her.

"Ask me their names," Idana told Jamis. Jamis shook her head, heart racing, an uneasy sensation crawling down her legs. "Ask."

Jamis ducked her head. She didn't want to look at her anymore. She already knew the answer. "No," Jamis said.

"Fine. I'll tell you. They're the Baughmans," Idana said, spelling the last name. "Sometime in the mid-twentieth century they anglicized it to Bachman."

Jamis continued to walk. Her particular story began here, in Jerome, with the bastard child of Idana Drake and Jacob Monihan. He survived and had his own children, creating the family tree she knew nothing about. Until now. Maybe she should do that DNA test she saw ads for all over social media. Idana took her hand and Jamis let her. She was her progeny.

"What do you want from me?" Jamis stopped at the end of the street, taking her hand from Idana. The desert was dark and she was tired. She wasn't sure how that was possible, since her physical body was somewhere else. Her thoughts must have been loud because Idana heard them.

"You think in these binary terms of past and present. Life and death. It's all really the same. We're standing in one place and there are filters over it," Idana said.

"Emma tried to tell me that too, but I still don't understand," Jamis said.

"It's not important that you do. It's just important that you're here," Idana said.

"You won't tell me what you want from me," Jamis said. She sat down with her back against the last building on the street. Oddly, Idana stooped next to her. She wasn't expecting her to join her. She scooted away from her. Idana might be her great-grandmother, four or five times removed, but she'd still seen her eat people's souls.

"I need you to help me break this cycle. What do you know about rituals for re-installment of souls?"

"Absolutely nothing because there is no such thing," Jamis said.

"That's not true so we'll need Baxter's help," Idana said.

"I thought I liked him, at first, but then there was something wrong with him," Jamis said.

"And you don't like him now?"

"Not since he showed up with a shotgun, no, I don't," Jamis said.

"He's a strange one. He doesn't matter though. You do. Let's go back and get it over with," Idana said and pulled Jamis up.

Jamis stumbled and looked up to see she was back on the hill with Levi and Baxter.

"What just happened? You were there, then you were gone, for just a minute, now you're back," Levi said. Baxter poked him in the back with the gun and he stopped moving toward her.

"Met my grandma," Jamis said. Levi said nothing, but his face paled. He'd lost weight since she met him and looked so tired. "You had to be there."

"Enough," Baxter said and pushed Levi forward. He took a flashlight from his back pocket. Jamis stood in the middle of a symbol, painstakingly constructed to look like the Ancient Flower of Life. The perfect geometry of the symbol was immediately visible, and she was upset she'd not noticed it before she stood in the middle of it.

"What do you think this is going to do?" It was the symbol spiritualists claimed spurred creation. Its lore included studies of sacred geometry which included the egg, fruit, and seed of life. It was also present in the folklore of ancient alchemy. The symbol was found throughout the ancient world, inscribed on temple walls in Egypt, Tibet, and South America. Some alternate archaeologists connected it to the lost empire of Atlantis. But why Baxter was using it was a mystery to her.

"I'm surprised you don't know," Baxter said.

"Did you learn this with your transpersonal psychology degree?" Jamis shifted away from the center of symbol.

"Don't you dare move or I'll shoot him," Baxter said, pointing the gun at Levi. She needed to stall him, to engage his ego to discover what he was doing.

"It's the Ancient Flower of Life. Don't some in your world call this the Egg, Fruit, or Seed of life, like Da Vinci?"

"I'm impressed. You've heard of it," Baxter said.

"Yeah, of course. It's the foundation of a lot of modern metaphysical thought," Jamis said.

"It's more than that. When harnessed, with the right intention, it can break traumatic cycles, generate, channel, and transition energy. I built it years ago for Idana. It's how we feed her, anchor her here," Baxter said.

"You're telling me a symbol can do that?" Jamis didn't believe him and thought his explanation was delusional. But she just traveled through time with Idana, so what did she know about anything.

"Symbols are everything. They hold everything we take for granted together. From flags to constitutions. Principles and laws. It's all symbolic. It all requires we project our consciousness outward to attach to it," Baxter said.

"Well, that's just life. Everything is always changing, moving, impermanent. Stability is the greatest fraud ever," Jamis said.

"No. Death is. Idana is proof. When her journals were found, and that woman came to me, Idana came with her. Before then, I had no idea how magical and wonderful this universe could be," Baxter said. The delusional fool was in love with a woman who would eat his soul when he died. It was really sad.

Idana was back, standing next to Jamis but Baxter couldn't see her.

"How does she talk to you?" Jamis ignored Idana's presence.

"In my dreams. That's how she's always come to me," he said.

"Is that why you got your degree?"

"To understand states of consciousness, and I've done it," he said.

"I'll never scoff at transpersonal psychology again," Jamis said. Levi was inching away from the distracted Baxter. "But I still don't understand the Flower of Life."

"He doesn't either," Idana said to Jamis. "But I do. This symbol, constructed on the spot of my traumatic death, has allowed me to continuously recharge my soul. And now that you're here, it's going to reinstall my soul in this dimension."

"By eating the souls of people your minions butcher for you," Jamis said.

"Who are you talking to?" Baxter strode to the center of the circle to stand next to Jamis.

Jamis ignored him and faced Idana. "You killed your husband, your lover, and now you just arbitrarily participate in the murders of innocents and I should say, 'Gosh, Grandma, happy to meet you'?"

"Don't you see that all your strength comes from me? You survived and thrived because of what I gave you. Just like I did. It was a different time," Idana said. It was a different time. And all human ethics were constructs. Baxter was right about that. It's just Jamis liked some of them. Maybe if Jamis had lived her youth during Idana's time, she'd be as brutal and uncaring. But she didn't and couldn't.

"But what do you want from me? You've risked me to get me here. Yanked Levi along," Jamis said.

Baxter fired a shot in the air, furious at being ignored. "You will talk to me," he yelled at Jamis.

Levi came behind him and struck him in the head with a large block. Baxter dropped in the middle of the circle and blood ran from a cut in his scalp into the dirt.

"This is what I've wanted to do for years," Idana said with a laugh. The man in the hat arrived then, with a strong gust of wind. Jamis stumbled.

"He's coming," the man said and Jamis reached out to see if she could touch him. As her hand passed through his shoulder, his appearance changed. Jamis stared at him and recognized him from a flashback she shared with Idana. He was the man who warned her of the posse's arrival before she was hanged.

"Didn't she call you John?" Jamis tried to touch him again but could not. Somehow, just acknowledging him allowed some transformation.

"Yes," he said, voice low, tone confused.

"Just let go. Do you see a light?" The man stared over Jamis's shoulder and nodded. "Go to it." His visage changed, solidified, and he looked alive.

"It's my brother and mom," he said and walked by her and was gone.

"You're a soft touch, Jamis," Idana said.

Levi heard it. "Holy shit. Is that her? I think I just heard something," he said.

"Let's finish off Baxter," Idana said.

"You can do it yourself," Jamis said.

"It's not time yet. I need you to break the cycle for me," Idana said.

"This is where I was supposed to take you," Levi said. He'd dropped the rock and was standing at the edge of the cliff. "It wasn't that building at all."

"All of creation begins in fire and chaos. It's the natural state of the universe," Idana said.

"You know what else is natural? Viruses. But I'm a huge fan of vaccines," Jamis said.

"Just help me," Idana said.

"How? I don't even know how, and I can't do it because I think you're kinda evil, even though I really like you," Jamis said, legs buckling. She was so tired.

"Why me?" Levi put an arm around Jamis's waist to steady her.

"Bad luck, and poor genetics, like me. We're a couple of unwanted kids who fled our tortured childhoods with some decency. Idana thinks that makes us the same," Jamis said.

"Maybe it does," Levi said.

"You are going to help me," Idana said and disappeared.

"That lady is scary," Levi said. A long bang went off and something flashed by Jamis's eyes. Levi dropped, blood spilling from the left side of his torso. He grabbed at his chest, blood running between his fingertips. "I've been shot," he said and then his eyes rolled back into his head.

Gabe stood at the gate of cemetery, gun pointed.

"Are you kidding me? Baxter shot you," Jamis yelled.

"Vest," he said and fired again. Jamis ducked and ran for Baxter's gun in the middle of the symbol. Gabe followed and stood just inside the symbol. Jamis and Gabe stood facing each other, guns raised. "Bet I'm a better shot," Gabe said, finger on the trigger.

Jamis searched for an appropriate response and found none. She was so tired. Levi was shot. America had too many guns. She didn't even know how to shoot the one she was holding. She might never see Johnna again. Her great-grandma was a crazy, soul eating poltergeist who manipulated men into doing awful things for her. It was enough to make any sane person just give in, toss in the towel.

"Fuck it," Jamis said.

"What?" Gabe was confused and for just a second, shifted his gun down. When he did, something struck him in the neck. It was dark and Jamis didn't know what it was. For a confused moment, she thought it was a rabid bat because that would make her adventure complete. But then Gabe dropped his gun and his knees buckled and he fell flat on his face. Jamis stared at him.

"Jamis," she heard, followed by rustling footsteps. Lights from cars came barreling down the road into the cemetery and let her follow the voice. Only one person moved that gracefully over rocks and through tumbleweeds.

"Johnna," she yelled and tried to step toward her, but her legs gave out. Johnna was there, arms around her, hands on her face, kissing her, tears in her eyes.

"Levi," Jamis said, pointing.

Other people were there too. Sapphire arrived, followed Jamis's finger, and was on her hands and knees at Levi's side. "He's hurt," she yelled at the cop cars swarming the scene, lights flashing.

"Someone tie up Gabe because he's a piece of shit," Jamis yelled and Johnna hugged her. "Hey, how'd he fall?"

"I shot him with a tranquilizer dart I keep in my truck for cougars," Johnna said.

"You shot him with a dart?" Jamis let Johnna turn her around so she could lean against her. Johnna's arms felt like heaven.

"Yes," Johnna said, kissing Jamis's forehead.

"How'd you find me? When did you get here?"

"Sapphire called as soon as she got free. I drove through the night. Blaire and Devon told us where you were last. I was out, on foot, and I heard a gunshot and ran toward it," Johnna said.

"Thank God you're in shape because I'm not. You found me," Jamis said.

"I did. You're safe now," Johnna said. The cops lifted an unconscious Gabe onto a stretcher and handcuffed him to it. Baxter sat up under the ministrations of paramedics.

"Handcuff him too," Jamis yelled and then closed her eyes. When she opened them, paramedics were bent over Levi. They were connecting an IV. He'd be okay. He had to be okay. The cops had Baxter on his feet, hands behind his back. "He's a son of bitch! I think he ruptured my eardrum," Jamis yelled at Baxter as he walked by. She tried to kick dirt on him.

"Can you stand?" Jamis nodded and Johnna helped her up, arm around her waist, one holding her hand on her shoulder. Vera walked toward them. "No questions until she's treated at a hospital," Johnna said, pushing past her. Johnna took Jamis to a cop car, sat her on the passenger seat, and held her face in her hands. She waved and Carmen arrived. "Wait with her while I get the truck."

"Again, ghost hunter," Carmen said. Jamis lifted her hands in small cheer gesture.

"My grandma eats souls," Jamis said.

"I trust we'll talk more about that later," Carmen said.

"Yeah," Jamis closed her eyes. She was no longer in the front seat of the car. It was day and the air was cool.

"I think you did it," Idana said, now dressed in a light blue dress.

"Broke your cycle? But how?"

"You're my progeny and you didn't die there. People came to help you. Love saved you," Idana said.

"It didn't save you because you're mean," Jamis said.

"You and I are only different in degrees."

"I'm nothing like you," Jamis said.

"We'll see," Idana said.

"Are you free now or what? Going to move on to what comes next? Is this our grand good-bye?" Jamis was angry. How did she come from such a monster?

"Why would I move on? I'm just getting started here. I'll see you soon," Idana said and blew Jamis a kiss before she disappeared.

Jamis opened her eyes as Johnna returned to her. "You look so tired," Jamis said, touching her face and the dark circles under her eyes. "I'm so sorry."

"We're finding you a desk job," Johnna said and Jamis nodded.

"I mean, she stopped a serial killer this time," Carmen said. Jamis tried to hold up her arms and flex her muscles but was too tired.

"Come on. Let's get you down to Cottonwood to the hospital," Johnna said, helping her into the front seat of the truck. Sapphire and Carmen joined them. The ambulance pulled away, lights blaring, as they raced Levi there as well.

CHAPTER TWENTY

Jamis rolled over in bed and put her arm around Johnna's waist and scooted closer. The hotel room they took in Cottonwood a few days before had become a comfortable retreat from the insanity of the events of the previous week. Johnna laced Jamis's fingers with her own and pulled her hand up between her breasts, snuggling in tighter.

"I really thought you were going to die," Johnna said.

"I really thought I was too," Jamis said.

"All I could think is that there was no way life could be so awful to take you from me."

Jamis kissed her neck and rested her face there, breathing her in. "Do you always travel with a tranquilizer gun is what I want to know." Jamis sought to lighten the mood. She'd been exhausted the two previous days, sleeping most of them away. She'd wakened only to eat and drink.

"I have many secrets," Johnna said with a smile.

"And talents. The IVs you keep giving me are amazing," Jamis said. Somehow, Johnna managed to get extra bags of IV solution from the hospital and administered them directly to Jamis.

"You're not all that different from a dog," Johnna said.

"I know that's a compliment from you," Jamis said, grabbing her side to tickle. They rolled around together, laughing, each struggling for the upper hand. "I give," Jamis said, throwing her arms back in defeat.

Johnna sat up next to her and lifted her shirt to touch her ribs. "Still okay?" She checked her other side and then pulled her shirt back down and looked at her cuts and bruises.

"Thanks for taking care of me, Doc," Jamis said. Johnna curled up against her side, head on her shoulder.

Idana arrived in the corner of the room at just that moment, and Jamis jerked upward, startling Johnna. Idana just waved and flickered away again. It was the first time Jamis had seen her since she'd somehow helped her break the cycle of her karmic punishment.

"Idana," Jamis said.

"Here?" Johnna's hand was on her back, right between her shoulder blades and its warmth calmed her.

"Yeah," Jamis said and relaxed back into the bed. Johnna curled back up against her, hand on her stomach. "I'm sorry."

"For what?" Johnna touched her face gently with her hand.

"For who I am as a human," Jamis said.

Johnna laughed and shifted to stand. "I love you just as you are, Jamis Bachman. Now let's get dressed, eat some food, and visit Levi."

"We might have to take him home," Jamis said.

Johnna was halfway to the bathroom and stopped to look at her. "Levi?"

Jamis shrugged. "He doesn't have anyone else."

Johnna smiled. "You're wrong. He has us."

"The last few days have been such a blur," Jamis said.

"The cops came by. They got Gabe and Baxter. More court cases for you to testify in. But I guess they're set to solve more than a dozen missing persons cases from the sixties through the nineties because of you. And six present day murders," Johnna said.

"Ghost hunter by night, crime fighter by day," Jamis said.

"Do you want a cape?"

"Would I look good in one? Would it go with my eyes? I have a reputation, you know," Jamis said.

❖

Johnna and Jamis waited by Levi's bed. The bullet just missed his artery, but he still needed surgery to repair the damage. He opened his eyes and smiled.

"Hey," he said.

"Thanks for saving me," Jamis said.

"I brought Baxter right to you."

"He would have found me anyway. I survived because of you," she said.

Johnna shifted forward. "I'm Johnna, Levi. It's nice to meet you."

"Are you her wife?"

Jamis coughed and gasped and Johnna smiled. "Not yet. Tell her to ask."

"I will," he said with a smile.

"Jamis tells me you're a little down on your luck. If you want to come back north with us, I have a friend who's renting out a small apartment above her garage and looking for some help around her ranch. You can ride with us."

"Really?" He was probably about twenty-one, but he looked so young, innocent, and eager.

"Yeah," Johnna said, and warmth spread through Jamis's chest. Johnna was the ultimate bleeding heart. Had a corner on the market. Carmen and Lucy knocked on the door and set flowers and a balloon on the table for him. Lucy unwrapped a plate of food and shifted the bed cart over his lap. Levi sat up, eager for the food. Only Sapphire and Sam were missing, but Johnna had insisted she return home once she'd arrived to take care of Jamis.

"Johnna said I can come back to Sage Creek. Got some work lined up for me," Levi told Lucy and Carmen, tone proud. Carmen smiled.

"It's a good place for misfits like us," Jamis said to him.

About the Author

Jen Jensen lives in Phoenix, Arizona, with a pack of rescued senior dogs, lovely family, and friends, and spends too much time reading books.

Books Available from Bold Strokes Books

A Woman to Treasure by Ali Vali. An ancient scroll isn't the only treasure Levi Montbard finds as she starts her hunt for the truth—all she has to do is prove to Yasmine Hassani that there's more to her than an adventurous soul. (978-1-63555-890-6)

Before. After. Always. by Morgan Lee Miller. Still reeling from her tragic past, Eliza Walsh has sworn off taking risks, until Blake Navarro turns her world right-side up, making her question if falling in love again is worth it. (978-1-63555-845-6)

Bet the Farm by Fiona Riley. Lauren Calloway's luxury real estate sale of the century comes to a screeching halt when dairy farm heiress, and one-night stand, Thea Boudreaux calls her bluff. (978-1-63555-731-2)

Cowgirl by Nance Sparks. The last thing Aren expects is to fall for Carol. Sharing her home is one thing, but sharing her heart means sharing the demons in her past and risking everything to keep Carol safe. (978-1-63555-877-7)

Give In to Me by Elle Spencer. Gabriela Talbot never expected to sleep with her favorite author—certainly not after the scathing review she'd given Whitney Ainsworth's latest book. (978-1-63555-910-1)

Hidden Dreams by Shelley Thrasher. A lethal virus and its resulting vision send Texan Barbara Allan and her lovely guide, Dara, on a journey up Cambodia's Mekong River in search of Barbara's mother's mystifying past. (978-1-63555-856-2)

In the Spotlight by Lesley Davis. For actresses Cole Calder and Eris Whyte, their chance at love runs out fast when a fan's adoration turns to obsession. (978-1-63555-926-2)

Origins by Jen Jensen. Jamis Bachman is pulled into a dangerous mystery that becomes personal when she learns the truth of her origins as a ghost hunter. (978-1-63555-837-1)

Pursuit: A Victorian Entertainment by Felice Picano. An intelligent, handsome, ruthlessly ambitious young man who rose from the slums to become the right-hand man of the Lord Exchequer of England will stop at nothing as he pursues his Lord's vanished wife across Continental Europe. (978-1-63555-870-8)

Unrivaled by Radclyffe. Zoey Cohen will never accept second place in matters of the heart, even when her rival is a career, and Declan Black has nothing left to give of herself or her heart. (978-1-63679-013-8)

A Fae Tale by Genevieve McCluer. Dovana comes to terms with her changing feelings for her lifelong best friend and fae, Roze. (978-1-63555-918-7)

Accidental Desperados by Lee Lynch. Life is clobbering Berry, Jaudon, and their long romance. The arrival of directionless baby dyke MJ doesn't help. Can they find their passion again—and keep it? (978-1-63555-482-3)

Always Believe by Aimée. Greyson Walsden is pursuing ordination as an Anglican priest. Angela Arlingham doesn't believe in God. Do they follow their vocation or their hearts? (978-1-63555-912-5)

Best of the Wrong Reasons by Sander Santiago. For Fin Ness and Orion Starr, it takes a funeral to remind them that love is worth living for. (978-1-63555-867-8)

Courage by Jesse J. Thoma. No matter how often Natasha Parsons and Tommy Finch clash on the job, an undeniable attraction simmers just beneath the surface. Can they find the courage to change so love has room to grow? (978-1-63555-802-9)

I Am Chris by R Kent. There's one saving grace to losing everything and moving away. Nobody knows her as Chrissy Taylor. Now Chris can live who he truly is. (978-1-63555-904-0)

The Princess and the Odium by Sam Ledel. Jastyn and Princess Aurelia return to Venostes and join their families in a battle against the dark force to take back their homeland for a chance at a better tomorrow. (978-1-63555-894-4)

The Queen Has a Cold by Jane Kolven. What happens when the heir to the throne isn't a prince or a princess? (978-1-63555-878-4)

The Secret Poet by Georgia Beers. Agreeing to help her brother woo Zoe Blake seemed like a good idea to Morgan Thompson at first…until she realizes she's actually wooing Zoe for herself… (978-1-63555-858-6)

You Again by Aurora Rey. For high school sweethearts Kate Cormier and Sutton Guidry, the second chance might be the only one that matters. (978-1-63555-791-6)

Coming to Life on South High by Lee Patton. Twenty-one-year-old gay virgin Gabe Rafferty's first adult decade unfolds as an unpredictable journey into sex, love, and livelihood. (978-1-63555-906-4)

Love's Falling Star by B.D. Grayson. For country music megastar Lochlan Paige, can love conquer her fear of losing the one thing she's worked so hard to protect? (978-1-63555-873-9)

Love's Truth by C.A. Popovich. Can Lynette and Barb make love work when unhealed wounds of betrayed trust and a secret could change everything? (978-1-63555-755-8)

Next Exit Home by Dena Blake. Home may be where the heart is, but for Harper Sims and Addison Foster, is the journey back worth the pain? (978-1-63555-727-5)

Not Broken by Lyn Hemphill. Falling in love is hard enough—even more so for Rose who's carrying her ex's baby. (978-1-63555-869-2)

The Noble and the Nightingale by Barbara Ann Wright. Two women on opposite sides of empires at war risk all for a chance at love. (978-1-63555-812-8)

What a Tangled Web by Melissa Brayden. Clementine Monroe has the chance to buy the café she's managed for years, but Madison LeGrange swoops in and buys it first. Now Clementine is forced to work for the enemy and ignore her former crush. (978-1-63555-749-7)

A Far Better Thing by JD Wilburn. When needs of her family and wants of her heart clash, Cass Halliburton is faced with the ultimate sacrifice. (978-1-63555-834-0)

Body Language by Renee Roman. When Mika offers to provide Jen erotic tutoring, will sex drive them into a deeper relationship or tear them apart? (978-1-63555-800-5)

Carrie and Hope by Joy Argento. For Carrie and Hope loss brings them together but secrets and fear may tear them apart. (978-1-63555-827-2)

Death's Prelude by David S. Pederson. In this prequel to the Detective Heath Barrington Mystery series, Heath discovers that first love changes you forever and drives you to become the person you're destined to be. (978-1-63555-786-2)

Ice Queen by Gun Brooke. School counselor Aislin Kennedy wants to help standoffish CEO Susanna Durr and her troubled teenage daughter become closer—even if it means risking her own heart in the process. (978-1-63555-721-3)

Masquerade by Anne Shade. In 1925 Harlem, New York, a notorious gangster sets her sights on seducing Celine, and new lovers Dinah and Celine are forced to risk their hearts, and lives, for love. (978-1-63555-831-9)

Royal Family by Jenny Frame. Loss has defined both Clay's and Katya's lives, but guarding their hearts may prove to be the biggest heartbreak of all. (978-1-63555-745-9)

Share the Moon by Toni Logan. Three best friends, an inherited vincyard and a resident ghost come together for fun, romance and a touch of magic. (978-1-63555-844-9)

Spirit of the Law by Carsen Taite. Attorney Owen Lassiter will do almost anything to put a murderer behind bars, but can she get past her reluctance to rely on unconventional help from the alluring Summer Byrne and keep from falling in love in the process? (978-1-63555-766-4)

The Devil Incarnate by Ali Vali. Cain Casey has so much to live for, but enemies who lurk in the shadows threaten to unravel it all. (978-1-63555-534-9)

His Brother's Viscount by Stephanie Lake. Hector Somerville wants to rekindle his illicit love affair with Viscount Wentworth, but he must overcome one problem: Wentworth still loves Hector's brother. (978-1-63555-805-0)

Journey to Cash by Ashley Bartlett. Cash Braddock thought everything was great, but it looks like her history is about to become her right now. Which is a real bummer. (978-1-63555-464-9)

Liberty Bay by Karis Walsh. Wren Lindley's life is mired in tradition and untouched by trends until social media star Gina Strickland introduces an irresistible electricity into her off-the-grid world. (978-1-63555-816-6)

Scent by Kris Bryant. Nico Marshall has been burned by women in the past wanting her for her money. This time, she's determined to win Sophia Sweet over with her charm. (978-1-63555-780-0)

Shadows of Steel by Suzie Clarke. As their worlds collide and their choices come back to haunt them, Rachel and Claire must figure out how to stay together and most of all, stay alive. (978-1-63555-810-4)

The Clinch by Nicole Disney. Eden Bauer overcame a difficult past to become a world champion mixed martial artist, but now rising star and dreamy bad girl Brooklyn Shaw is a threat both to Eden's title and her heart. (978-1-63555-820-3)

The Last First Kiss by Julie Cannon. Kelly Newsome is so ready for a tropical island vacation, but she never expects to meet the woman who could give her her last first kiss. (978-1-63555-768-8)

The Mandolin Lunch by Missouri Vaun. Despite their immediate attraction, everything about Garet Allen says short-term, and Tess Hill refuses to consider anything less than forever. (978-1-63555-566-0)

Thor: Daughter of Asgard by Genevieve McCluer. When Hannah Olsen finds out she's the reincarnation of Thor, she's thrown into a world of magic and intrigue, unexpected attraction, and a mystery she's got to unravel. (978-1-63555-814-2)

Veterinary Technician by Nancy Wheelton. When a stable of horses is threatened Val and Ronnie must work together against the odds to save them, and maybe even themselves along the way. (978-1-63555-839-5)